MACK & MABEL

A Musical Love Story

Book by MICHAEL STEWART

Music and Lyrics by JERRY HERMAN

SAMUEL FRENCH, INC.

25 West 45th Street   NEW YORK 10036
7623 Sunset Boulevard   HOLLYWOOD 90046
LONDON   *TORONTO*

A set of orchestral parts with piano conductor score and principal chorus books will be loaned two months prior to the production ONLY on receipt of the royalty quoted for all performances, the rental fee and a refundable deposit. The deposit will be refunded on the safe return to SAMUEL FRENCH, INC. of all material loaned for the production.

Stock royalty quoted on application to SAMUEL FRENCH, INC.

CAUTION: All other rights in this play, including professional recording, motion picture, recitation, lecturing, public reading, radio and television broadcasting, and the rights of translation into foreign languages, are strictly reserved, permission for which must be secured in writing from the authors' representatives: Linden & Deutsch (for Michael Stewart) 110 East 59th Street, New York, N.Y. 10022; William Morris Agency, Inc. (for Jerry Herman) Attention: Jerome Talbert, 1350 Avenue of the Americas, New York, N.Y. 10019.

Vocal selections are available at $6.95 per copy, plus postage.

Printed in U.S.A.

ISBN 0 573 68074 4

OPENING NIGHT OCTOBER 6, 1974

MAJESTIC THEATRE

DAVID MERRICK

presents

ROBERT   BERNADETTE
PRESTON   PETERS

in

MACK & MABEL

a musical love story

Book by   *Music and Lyrics by*

MICHAEL STEWART   JERRY HERMAN

Also Starring

LISA
KIRK

with

JERRY DODGE   CHRISTOPHER MURNEY   TOM BATTEN
BERT MICHAELS NANCY EVERS ROBERT FITCH STANLEY SIMMONDS

and

JAMES MITCHELL
In Association with EDWIN H. MORRIS

Scenic Design	*Costume Design*	*Lighting Design*
ROBIN WAGNER	PATRICIA ZIPPRODT	THARON MUSSER

Musical Director and *Vocal Arrangements* DONALD PIPPIN	*Orchestrations* PHILIP J. LANG	*Incidental and* *Dance Music* JOHN MORRIS

Associate Choreographer BUDDY SCHWAB	*Production Supervisor* LUCIA VICTOR

Associate Producer JACK SCHLISSEL	*Based on an idea by* LEONARD SPIGELGASS

Hair Stylist TED AZAR
Original Cast Album by ABC Records

Directed and Choreographed by

GOWER CHAMPION

MACK & MABEL, a musical based on an idea by Leonard
Spigelgass. Book by Michael Stewart; music and lyrics by
Jerry Herman; setting by Robin Wagner; costumes by Pa-
tricia Zipprodt lighting by Tharon Musser; musical director
and vocal arrangements, Donald Pippin; orchestrations, Philip
J. Lang; incidental and dance music by John Morris; produc-
tion supervisor, Lucia Victor; hair stylist, Ted Azar; directed
and choreographed by Gower Champion; associate chore-
ographer, Buddy Schwab; production stage manager, Marnel
Sumner. Presented by David Merrick in association with
Edwin H. Morris; Jack Schlissel, associate producer. At the
Majestic Theater, 245 West 44th Street, New York, N.Y., on
October 6, 1974.

CHARACTERS

EDDIE, the Watchman .... *Stanley Simmonds*

MACK SENNETT .... *Robert Preston*

LOTTIE AMES .... *Lisa Kirk*

ELLA .... *Nancy Evers*

FREDDIE .... *Roger Bigelow*

CHARLIE MULDOON .... *Christopher Murney*

WALLY .... *Robert Fitch*

FRANK WYMAN .... *Jerry Dodge*

MABEL NORMAND .... *Bernadette Peters*

MR. KLEIMAN .... *Tom Batten*

MR. FOX .... *Bert Michaels*

IRIS, the Wardrobe Mistress .... *Marie Santell*

WILLIAM DESMOND TAYLOR .... *James Mitchell*

PHYLLIS FOSTER .... *Cheryl Armstrong*

SERGE .... *Frank Root*

5

SCENES AND MUSICAL NUMBERS

Scene 1:   The Sennett Studios, 1938
MOVIES WERE MOVIES .... *Mack*

Scene 2:   The Brooklyn Studio, 1911
LOOK WHAT HAPPENED TO MABEL .. *Mabel, Wally,*
Charlie, Frank and Grips

Scene 3:   Mack's Office, Brooklyn
BIG TIME .... *Lottie and the Family*

Scene 4:   En Route to California
I WON'T SEND ROSES .... *Mack*
REPRISE: I WON'T SEND ROSES .... *Mabel*

Scene 5:   Los Angeles, 1912
I WANNA MAKE THE WORLD LAUGH .... *Mack and*
the Company

Scene 6:   On the Set
REPRISE: I WANNA MAKE THE WORLD LAUGH ..
Mack and Company

Scene 7:   The Orchid Room of the Hollywood Hotel, 1919
WHEREVER HE AIN'T .... *Mabel and Waiters*

Scene 8:   On the Set
HUNDREDS OF GIRLS ...... *Mack and Bathing Beauties*

Scene 9:   Mack's New Office, 1923

Scene 10:   Studio Early Next Morning
WHEN MABEL COMES IN THE ROOM ...... *Company*
HIT 'EM ON THE HEAD .... *Mack, Kleiman,*
Fox, and Kops

Scene 11:   A Pier, New York
TIME HEALS EVERYTHING .... *Mabel*

Scene 12:   "Vitagraph Varieties of 1929" and the terrace of
William Desmond Taylor's home
TAP YOUR TROUBLES AWAY .... *Lottie and Girls*

Scene 13:   Mack's Office—then Mabel's Home
I PROMISE YOU A HAPPY ENDING .... *Mack*

Scene 14:   The Sennett Studio, 1938

6

Mack & Mabel

ACT ONE

SCENE 1

*OVERTURE ends and in the darkness we hear the sound of
somebody pounding with his fist on a heavy steel door.
The SAFETY CURTAIN has slowly been rising through
this and as pounding continues we find ourselves amid the
girders, booms, darkened spotlight, etc., of a MOTION
PICTURE SOUND STAGE. The time is two in the
morning, the year is 1938.*

*The pounding has become more insistent and now an angry
VOICE shouts, "Open up, dammit!" We see a flashlight
flicker as a WATCHMAN hurries to door and asks "Who
is it?" "Me, you idiot," the VOICE answers, "now open
up!" The WATCHMAN unlatches the door, slides it back,
and we see MACK SENNETT framed in the hard white light
of the studio street lamp outside. He is a big burly man,
now in his late fifties, a bit drunk.*

WATCHMAN. (*As MACK starts past him.*) I'm sorry, Mr.
Sennett, I didn't know it was you, besides the rule says
no-one gets in after midnight, I know that don't mean you
but rules is rules and . . .

MACK. Light.

WATCHMAN. Hah?

MACK. How do you expect me to see in this dump, get some
light on!

WATCHMAN. The work light's on, Mr. Sennett, that's all is
allowed at night, that's the rules . . .

MACK. Screw the rules, til tomorrow noon this is *my* studio
and I want it light! (*Lurching past protesting WATCHMAN to
light board.*) . . . The way I made it, and kept it, and God-
damn it the way I'm leaving it! (*He has pulled lever and a
beam of light comes crashing down.*) Where's my chair?

WATCHMAN. With them others, Mr. Sennett. They're going
up to the prop room. (*As MACK starts for chairs.*) . . . No
one's supposed to touch them.

7

MACK. No one's not me, now get outa here. (WATCHMAN *doesn't move.*) I said get out! (WATCHMAN *hesitates, then mumbles "Yessir" and starts to light board right.* MACK *has taken battered director's chair from pile, we see the name Sennett in faded letters across the back. He stops, turns to us.*) What do you know about making movies? Well let Sennett tell you. Not a God-damn thing! (*He puts chair down in beam of light and continues.*) . . . Go on, take over this dump, I don't give a damn, I had what I wanted out of it. But don't tell me you're taking it over to make movies, I'm Sennett, I know the difference! Oh you'll make money with the crap you grind out . . . which we haven't in the past five years, have we Mr. Kleiman . . . but that's because some sonofabitch with a victrola's back of the screen cranking his little heart out and Jolson talks, Swanson talks, Rin-Tin-Tin talks and it still ain't movies! (*As he slumps into chair.*) Hey, whadda ya' gonna do five years from now when they're tired of talkies, whadda ya' gonna give 'em then? Colors? Or a new-size screen? Or bare butts and dirty words? Go on, try all the tricks you can think of it's still not gonna be worth one reel of Birth of a Nation, not one frame of Chaplin, not one eighth of a quarter of an inch of my Mabel . . . (*Suddenly.*) Cut that light!

WATCHMAN. You just put it on, Mr. Sennett . . .

MACK. Cut it! (*And the Stage is plunged into blackness as* MACK *softly repeats.*) My Mabel. (*MUSIC of a tinkly piano starts up in distance as he continues.*) Hey, kid, I'm here. Like a real hero, in the nick of time, with that big Sennett finish I promised! Yeah, I know, it's old hat, they don't give 'em those happy endings anymore . . . but what do they know about making movies? (*Softly.*) Like I told you. Not a God-damn thing. (*And he sings.*)

MOVIES WERE MOVIES WHEN YOU PAID A DIME
    TO ESCAPE
CHEERING THE HERO AND HISSING THE MAN
    IN THE CAPE
ROMANCE AND ACTION AND THRILLS
PARDNER THERE'S GOLD IN THEM HILLS
MOVIES WERE MOVIES WHEN DURING THE
    TITLES YOU'D KNOW
YOU'D GET A HAPPY ENDING
DOZENS OF BLUNDERING COPS IN A
    THUNDERING CHASE

GETTING A BANG OUT OF LEMON MERINGUE IN
   THE FACE
BANDITS ATTACKING A TRAIN
ONE LITTLE TRAMP WITH A CANE
MOVIES WERE MOVIES WERE MOVIES WHEN I
   RAN THE SHOW
      (*Lights begin to come slowly up as* MACK *continues:*)
MOVIES WERE MOVIES WHEN PAULINE WAS
   TIED TO THE TRACK
AFTER SHE TRUDGED THROUGH THE ICE WITH
   A BABE ON HER BACK
GIRLS AT THE SEASHORE WOULD STAND
ALL IN A ROW IN THE SAND
ROLLING THEIR STOCKINGS AN INCH AND A
   QUARTER BELOW
THE LINE OF DECENCY
AND SWANSON AND KEATON AND DRESSLER
   AND WILLIAM S. HART
NO ONE PRETENDED THAT WHAT WE WERE
   DOING WAS ART
WE HAD SOME GUTS AND SOME LUCK
BUT WE WERE JUST MAKIN' A BUCK
MOVIES WERE MOVIES WERE MOVIES WHEN I
   RAN THE SHOW!

   (*By now LIGHTS are halfway up and as* MACK *continues* FIGURES *start out of shadows and onto the Stage.* ACTORS *in costumes,* GRIPS *carrying set pieces and an old hand-cranked movie camera,* LADY *in elaborate hat of period pounding away at an upright piano, a bustle of activity as he sings:*)

SWANSON AND KEATON AND DRESSLER AND
   WILLIAM S. HART
NO ONE PRETENDED THAT WHAT WE WERE
   DOING WAS ART
WE HAD SOME GUTS AND SOME LUCK
BUT WE WERE JUST MAKIN' A BUCK
MOVIES WERE MOVIES WERE *MOVIES* . . .
WHEN I RAN THE SHOW!

   (*By now LIGHTS up full, Stage crowded with* ACTORS, GRIPS, *etc.* MACK, *in shirtsleeves, behind hand-cranked camera as we find ourselves. . . .*)

ACT ONE

SCENE 2

In MACK'S *first studio in Brooklyn, 1911.* GRIPS *have set up tubs, mangles, clothes-lines that make up Acme Hand Laundry, Est. 1901, Mrs. R. O'Flaherty Prop.* LOTTIE AMES *in golden-haired wig tied to a tub as* MACK *shouts.*

MACK. . . . Plead, dammit! He's just threatened to kill you, set fire to the laundry and put your baby through the mangle, so don't just whimper, you cow, plead!

LOTTIE. How can I plead when I'm dying of starvation, I haven't had a bite since six this morning, Mack, for God's sake, wait til my sandwich comes!

MACK. Cut! (*Crossing to* LOTTIE.) Look, you broken-down hoofer, in ten minutes that sun goes behind those clouds, either we're done by then or you'll be back with that lousy vaudeville act I found you in!

LOTTIE. Mack, I'm weak, I'm gonna die . . .

MACK. Fine. Only do it when the sun goes behind the clouds.

FRANK. (*About fifteen, carrying stack of newspapers.*) I'll bring you something, Miss Ames!

MACK. Frank, you stick to delivering papers. Alright, Ella, give us some music, I'm gonna get this one! (*And* ELLA *starts banging away at the upright as* MACK *gets behind camera and bellows directions.*) . . . Okay Freddie, you see she won't tell you where the money is so you get an idea. The baby! Either she coughs up the dough or you put the kid through the wringer. Cut to a title here . . . "Bring out the safe or I'll wring out the waif!" Lottie, you see him take the baby so you break loose and grab the other end, *easy,* it's a baby not God-damn taffy, Wally, this is where you come in. (WALLY *starts on dressed like a tramp with oversized shoes.*) That's it, the baby first! (WALLY *grabs it, doesn't know what to do with it, shoves it in his pants.*) Now take care of Freddie. (*A kick in the pants.*) Now Lottie, help 'er up and go for the clinch. Get the baby in there! (*He fishes it out.*) Alright now hold it! I want a good long one, you, Lottie, and the kid. One, two, three, four . . .

GIRL. (*Who has marched in between them through front door of laundry set.*) Hot knockwurst on a roll, fifteen cents.

MACK. Who the hell are you?

GIRL. From Schultz's delicatessen, you sent out, hot knock-wurst on a roll, fifteen . . .

MACK. Get outa here, can't you see we're shooting!

GIRL. (LOTTIE *has meanwhile handed her the baby, grabbed sandwich, and started eating.*) Not til I get my fifteen cents, she's eating my sandwich . . .

MACK. Andy get her the hell outa here!

ANDY. (*One of the* GRIPS, *as she repeats* "Not til I get my fifteen . . .") Alright, kid, let's go. (*He grabs her by arm, the baby drops.*)

GIRL. . . . Oh I killed the baby!

ANDY. (*As she picks it up.*) C'mon, kid, I said let's go! (*He starts to pull her off,* GIRL *has had enough, winds up and lets him have it in gut with baby.*)

ELLA. (*As* ANDY *hits the floor.*) Mac, should I stop?

MACK. (*Suddenly making up his mind, running back to camera.*) No!! Keep playing! We're getting a free one! (*And he starts cranking as* GIRL *grabs sandwich back from* LOTTIE *and with knockwurst in one hand, baby in the other, stands off* GRIPS, LOTTIE, WALLY, FREDDIE, *knocking one down, tripping another, shoving a third into the tub, etc. Last line is hers as she stagggers back against the steam press [into which, unfortunately, she had put the baby] and gasps.*)

GIRL. Hot knockwurst on a roll . . . (*Taking out baby, now crushed flatter than a pancake. Near tears.*) Fifteen cents. (*End SEQUENCE,* MACK *is delighted.*)

MACK. Great! Call it All Washed Up and get it ready for release by Monday. The rest of you beat it and don't forget we start Beauty and the Buzzsaw tomorrow at six! You, get rid of that thing and come here. (GIRL *does not know where to dispose of flattened baby, finally rolls it up and puts it in her purse.* OTHERS *have started off as* MACK *continues.*) Now what's your name? (*She mutters something inaudibly.*) Speak up, dammit, I'm a busy man!

GIRL. (*Babbling away as* MACK *circles her.*) Mabel A. Normand, A. for Agnes after St. Agnes, you see my family's very religious and if I go back without the fifteen cents Schultz who I work for is gonna think I kept it and tell Father McCready and that's fifty Hail Mary's at least plus . . .

MACK. (*Clapping his hand over her mouth to still the torrent. To us:*) . . . There was something about her! Whatever she felt just popped right out for the eye to see and what the eye could see so could the camera! Sure she was a total amateur but I wasn't. And we'd be doing it my way. (*Releas-*

ing her.) Alright, A. for St. Agnes, get the hell out of here
and come back tomorrow at six. We'll screen that stuff I just
shot and if there's anything worthwhile on it . . . you're
gonna be in pictures. (*She starts to say something.*) Don't
bother to thank me, just beat it! (*She starts off.*) Wait a
minute! (*She stops.*) . . . Here's your fifteen cents.

MABEL. (*Looking at coins he hands her.*) That's two dimes.

MACK. Correct. You owe me a nickel. (*Exiting after last of*
GRIPS.) Andy, how quick can we get this printed up, I
want to run it tomorrow before we start shooting . . . (*And
he is gone.* MABEL *makes sure she's alone then bravely calls
out.*)

MABEL. Oh yeah, well I'm not coming! (*Getting bolder when
no one answers.*) I got a good job at Schultz's, only ten
hours a day, every other Sunday off, nearly six dollars a week
with tips, you keep your movies! And if you think I'm getting
up at six in the morning for anything except early Mass which
I don't happen to be going to tomorrow because I already happen to have went yesterday, you got another think coming!
And another thing, don't count on getting that nickel change
so quick unless you wanna sue you cheapskate and in case you
don't know my uncle happens to be Justice P.J. Rooney of the
First Federal Court of Brooklyn and all I have to do is . . .
(*LIGHTS have gone down through this and* ANDY *has come
on pushing hand-cranked projector, it is the next morning,
and* FRANK *and* WALLY *join him as he starts to crank film
and* MABEL *gasps as she suddenly sees herself on imaginary
screen out in audience.*) Jesus, Mary and Joseph! (*And she
sings.*)

MISS WAITRESS FROM FLATBUSH GET DOWN
    FROM UP THERE
DON'T YOU KNOW THAT YOU'RE OUT OF YOUR
    CLASS
MISS WAITRESS FROM FLATBUSH I HOPE YOU'RE
    AWARE
YOU'RE BEHAVING LIKE SOME LITTLE ASS
HEY MISS
WHAT'S THIS . . .

SEE THAT FASCINATING CREATURE
WITH PERFECTION STAMPED ON EVERY
    FEATURE
SHE WAS PLAIN LITTLE NELLIE
THE KID FROM THE DELI
BUT MOTHER OF GOD LOOK WHAT HAPPENED
    TO MABEL

FROM NOW ON THIS PILE OF FLESH'LL
BE CONSIDERED SOMETHIN' PRETTY SPECIAL
AND MISS B.L.T. DOWN
IS THE TOAST OF THE TOWN
MARY, AND JOSEPH . . . WHAT HAPPENED TO
  MABEL

EVERY GESTURE AND POSITION THAT SHE
  TAKES
IS SMART AND METICULOUS
TALK ABOUT THE MAGIC THAT THE CAMERA
  MAKES
BUT THIS IS RIDICULOUS . . .

HOLD YOUR TONGUE AND HOLD YOUR
  SNICKERS
FOR THE NEW ENCHANTRESS OF THE FLICKERS
IS THAT PLAIN LITTLE NELLIE
THE KID FROM THE DELI
SO RATTLE ME BEADS
LOOK WHAT HAPPENED TO MABEL!

  (MABEL's *excitement spreads to* WALLY, FRANK *and* ANDY
  as she continues.)

SOMEONE WHO WAS PLAIN AS MUTTON
ON THE SCREEN IS CUTER THAN A BUTTON
AND THE GIRL WITH THE PICKLES
WHO HUSTLED FOR NICKELS
IS SOMETHIN' TO SEE . . . LOOK WHAT
  HAPPENED TO MABEL

YESTERDAY A TIP COLLECTOR
BUT TODAY JUST TURN ON THAT PROJECTOR
AND MISS AVENOO R
IS A REGULAR STAR
MOTHER MACHREE LOOK WHAT HAPPENED TO
  MABEL

UP TO NOW I NEVER REALLY KNEW THAT I
COULD BE SO AMBITIOUS
BUT SUDDENLY I KNOW I HAVE TO SAY
  GOODBYE
TO BAGELS AND KNISHES

Frank, Wally and Andy.
OH ST. ALOYSIUS!
    Mabel.
I KNOW THAT YOU MIGHT THINK I'M BALMY
BUT THE QUEEN OF CORNED-BEEF AND SALAMI
IS A GLAMOROUS GODDESS
WHO'S BUSTING HER BODICE
OH JUMPIN' ST. JUDE
    Andy.
LOOK!
    Wally.
LOOK!
    Frank.
LOOK!
    Mabel.
LOOK WHAT HAPPENED TO MABEL!

(*And as* MUSIC *continues, complete with props and costume changes, we see bits of the first three two-reelers that* Mabel *makes. First* Beauty and the Buzzsaw, *then* The New Manicurist, *and finally* Rose and the Redskins *featuring a dummy horse which is rocked back and forth against a moving cylinder with painted flats of the Old West.* Frank, Wally, Andy, Freddie, *etc. work in these cameos with her. We finish with* Mabel *struggling to get up on the horse as* All Grips, Actors *sing.*)

    Grips and Actors.
SEE THAT FASCINATING CREATURE
WITH PERFECTION STAMPED ON EVERY
    FEATURE
SHE WAS PLAIN LITTLE NELLIE
THE KID FROM THE DELI
BUT MOTHER OF GOD LOOK WHAT HAPPENED
    TO MABEL

SOMEONE WHO WAS PLAIN AS MUTTON
ON THE SCREEN IS CUTER THAN A BUTTON
AND THE GIRL WITH THE PICKELS
WHO HUSTLED FOR NICKELS
IS SOMETHING TO SEE . . . LOOK WHAT
    HAPPENED TO MABEL

EVERY GESTURE AND POSITION THAT SHE
    TAKES
IS SMART AND METICULOUS

TALK ABOUT THE MAGIC THAT THE CAMERA
   MAKES
BUT THIS IS RIDICULOUS

MABEL.
HOLD YOUR TONGUE AND HOLD YOUR SNICKERS
FOR THE NEW ENCHANTRESS OF THE FLICKERS
IS THAT PLAIN LITTLE NELLIE
   MEN.
THAT PLAIN LITTLE NELLIE
   MABEL.
THE KID FROM THE DELI
   MEN.
THE KID FROM THE DELI
   MABEL.
SO RATTLE ME BEADS
   MEN.
LOOK, LOOK, LOOK
   MABEL.
LOOK WHAT HAPPENED TO . . .
   ALL.
MABEL!

(*End song, applause, an exhausted* MABEL *goes Off Right to
   eat a hasty lunch as* GRIPS *strike horse, etc., and we go
   to . . .*)

ACT ONE

SCENE 3

MACK, *who has come on through last of NUMBER, as he
   watches departing* MABEL.

   MACK. The hell with what happened to Mabel! (*Softly.*)
. . . Look what was happening to Mack. (*And MUSIC comes
up as he sings.*)
SOMEHOW THE CEILING
SEEMED A LITTLE HIGHER
FROM THE VERY MOMENT I SAW MABEL COME
   IN THE ROOM
IT FELT LIKE SOMEONE
LIT A ROARING FIRE . . .

(*Music fades.* MACK's *mood is suddenly interrupted by a* MAN *who strides angrily on, slams manuscript down on* MACK's *desk.*)

MAN. That ending! With Mabel up on the horse! That was *not* in my script!

MACK. (*With a sigh as he unwraps his lunch.*) Writers. And scripts. They'll kill this industry yet. (*To* WRITER.) . . . Get the hell outa here, can't you see I'm eating my lunch!

WRITER. It's right here in black and white! The horse throws the girl then they all get trampled by a stampede of enraged buffalo then there's an epilogue in heaven with all of them wearing wings because they're angels and *that's* what makes the allegory! Didn't you even read the script?

MACK. What for? No movie's worth making that can't be told out loud in five sentences.

WRITER. In that case, *Mr.* Sennett . . .

MACK. Yeah, well nice meeting you. (*As* WRITER *storms out, tossing script after him.*) And take your aggelory . . . Take this thing with you.

LOTTIE. (*Coming on as* WRITER *exits.*) Wait a minute, where you going . . . Harry! Mack, you didn't fire the last writer we had left, not today of all days! Now we'll never get out this place.

MACK. I said we'd get out and we will! Now calm down and have an egg . . . Peel it first! (*To us as* LOTTIE *nervously claws at the egg.*) Lottie was hell-bent on following the other movie companies to California and she was right. With Mabel's two-reelers selling the way they were we were turning out six a week and had orders for sixty! We needed space, sunshine, room to spread out! Which is why two backers were coming down that afternoon to decide whether to put up the cash for the move. (*As* ELLA *starts angrily on.*) Which commodity, as usual, we needed.

ELLA. Mack, you get that piano tuned or I quit! Two G's are busted, one E-flat is stuck, the C won't go down and the B won't come up!

FRANK. (*Coming on with shredded paper.*) I know it's yesterday's Times, Mr. Sennett, but they won't give you today's til you pay what you owe! It's all there, no pages missing, just a little wet where they wrapped up the fish.

WALLY. (*Coming up from behind.*) I gotta have that back salary, Mack! My landlady woulda' thrown me out already only we got the arrangement. But I can't go on much longer, she's nearly eighty. And a devil!

MABEL. (*Marching on from Right.*) I just found out! Other movie stars get paid!

MACK. Which is why Lottie felt that with two potential backers on the way maybe I shouldn't have canned the only writer we had left. (*As KLEIMAN and FOX start on from Up Left.*) But I told 'er two bums like that are only interested in the actors! Last thing they'd ask to meet are writers! Look at 'em . . . Couldn't spell cat between 'em. (*Crossing to meet them.*) Mr. Kleiman! Mr. Fox! Welcome to Mack Sennett's Keystone Motion Picture Studios, home of the screen's brightest stars! (*Indicating* MABEL *and* LOTTIE.) The greatest clowns! (WALLY.) The most brilliant music department! (ELLA.) . . . And the best director of comedy in movies today! Well, boys, what do you think of it?

KLEIMAN and FOX. (*Simultaneously.*) Where's the writers?

MACK. And the finest writing staff in the business, high school graduates every one of them, headed by their chief, that jewel in the crown of American literary talent . . . (MACK *has been looking around desperately through this, his eye finally lights on* NEWSPAPER KID.) W. Frank Wyman! Up till very recently with the New York Times. (FRANK *has been holding his stack of papers behind his back, now quietly drops them.*) Well, gentlemen, are you with us or not?

KLEIMAN. Hold on, Sennett, it's not as simple as all that! There are pros and cons to be aired, shortcomings to be weighed, factors to be taken into account, intangibles to be pondered and imponderables to be thoroughly discussed . . .

FOX. Exactly! (*Then.*) . . . But as soon as we do that the answer is yes.

SENNETT. (*As* WALLY *lets out yip of joy and* ELLA, LOTTIE *hug* FOX.) Gentlemen, you got a deal! Forget the imponderables, Mr. Kleiman, the important is to make movies the way we want to make 'em.

KLEIMAN. Cheap!

MACK. We'll work that out. Now we'll need three weeks to wind up production here, another day or two to divest ourselves of whatever personal relationships we've been foolish enough to maintain, then on . . . (*Calendar on his desk.*) May 16th, nineteen hundred and eleven . . . (*A deep breath.*) We leave.

LOTTIE. We leave Brooklyn.

MACK. And scrounging to make a buck.

WALLY. And bills.

LOTTIE. And dispossess notices.

MACK. And fighting with merchants for film and canvas and wood and nails . . .

FRANK. Leave 'em all in the dust!

ELLA. In the lurch!

MABEL. Watch our smoke!

LOTTIE. Mr. Kleiman, Mr. Fox, you are our two good angels.

WALLY. Our meal tickets.

MABEL. Our railroad fare.

KLEIMAN. Speaking of the cars, Mr. Sennett, I understand the day coach service is splendid on these transcontinental trains . . .

MACK. Our first class Pullman angels! No more small time, Mr. Kleiman!

MABEL. (*As MUSIC starts up.*) Not for me!

WALLY. Or me!

ELLA and FRANK. Or me!

KLEIMAN, Fox and LOTTIE. Or me!

MACK. (*Softly, passionately.*) . . . Not for us.

(*And as* OTHERS *start off to get their things,* LOTTIE *crosses to* MACK, *takes his hands, and sings.*)

LOTTIE.
THIS TIME IT'S THE BIG TIME
IN A SHORT TIME WE CAN BE
THE CHERRY ON THE TOP OF THE SUNDAE
THE SHINY STAR ON TOP OF THE TREE
SO YOU'D BETTER
GRAB IT WITH YOUR BOTH HANDS
WHEN THAT GREAT MOMENT ARRIVES
CAUSE THIS TIME IT'S THE BIG TIME
IT'S THE BIG TIME OF OUR LIVES

(MACK *goes off,* GRIPS *start crossing with cameras, props, etc., as* LOTTIE *continues.*)

THIS TIME IT'S THE EXTRA
IT'S THE SPECIAL, IT'S THE PLUS
THIS TIME WE WON'T SAY "THOSE LUCKY
    BASTARDS"
THIS TIME THOSE LUCKY BASTARDS ARE US
AIN'T WE SOMETHIN!
FAREWELL TO THE SMALL TIME
TO THE FLEA BAGS AND THE DIVES
CAUSE THIS TIME IT'S THE BIG TIME
IT'S THE BIG TIME OF OUR LIVES!

WALLY. (*Coming back with suitcase.*)
I'M GONNA BUY MYSELF A PIERCE-ARROW
AND WAVE TO ALL MY FANS IN THE STREETS
MABEL. (*With her suitcase.*)
I'M GONNA HAVE A MANSION LIKE PICKFORD'S
ELLA.
I'M GONNA SLEEP ON BLACK SATIN SHEETS
FRANK, KLEIMAN and FOX.
AND WE'LL RAISE MORE HELL, MAKE MORE
    HAY
THAN DECENT FELLAS SHOULD
BECAUSE THE GANG FROM KING'S HIGHWAY
ALL PLUS GRIPS.
IS GOING HOLLYWOOD!

(MACK *has returned with his suitcase, now gathers* ENTIRE
    FAMILY *around him as they sing.*)

FAMILY. (*A whisper at first, growing louder through chorus.*)
THIS TIME IT'S THE BIG TIME
AND IT'S HIGH TIME WE WERE SEEN
BY EV'RY DAPPER DUDE IN DAKOTA
ON EV'RY SCROUNGY NEIGHBORHOOD SCREEN
SO YOU'D BETTER
GRAB IT WITH YOUR BOTH HANDS
WHEN THAT GREAT MOMENT ARRIVES
CAUSE THIS TIME IT'S THE BIG TIME
IT'S THE BIG TIME OF OUR LIVES!

(*By now the mood is one of wild jubilation as with* GRIPS,
    WARDROBE LADY, *etc., they continue.*)

THIS TIME IT'S THE EXTRA
IT'S THE SPECIAL, IT'S THE PLUS
THIS TIME WE WON'T SAY "THOSE LUCKY
    BASTARDS"
THIS TIME THOSE LUCKY BASTARDS ARE US
AIN'T WE SOMETHIN!
IN EACH HUNDRED MILLION
THERE'S A HANDFUL THAT SURVIVES
AND THIS TIME WE'RE THAT HANDFUL
SO IT'S BYE BYE TO THOSE ONE-NIGHTS
THIS TIME IT'S THE KLEIG LIGHTS
IT'S THE BIG BIG BIG TIME OF OUR LIVES!

(*End NUMBER, applause, MUSIC picks up again as one
    by one they start Off Right carrying suitcases, hat-boxes,*

birdcages, etc. Last one off is LOTTIE *leaving* MACK *alone Down Right as* MUSIC *becomes softer, lights start down and we come up on . . .)*

ACT ONE

SCENE 4

The Observation Platform of a train. Through following MABEL *comes out onto platform, breathes in the night air, looks at the star-filled sky all around her, and smiles happily to herself.*

MACK. . . . The train had stopped, I remember that. One of those hick burgs somewhere in the desert with two lights and a water tower. I'd walked down from my car to the end of the train to get some air and Mabel was sitting alone on the observation platform. I suppose if you love someone there's always one moment in time when it all begins. I didn't have brains enough to figure it out till too many years later but it was that night for me. I remember she was talking to herself, making up some crazy poem the way kids do . . . (*He smiles.*) Oh, Desert! That was the name of it. Oh, Desert.

MABEL. Oh, Desert!

MACK. (*Shaking his head, repeating softly to himself.*) Oh, desert . . .

MABEL.
Oh great Desert with your ever-shifting sands,
It is I, Mabel, who is crossing you
Astride your ever-shifting bosom . . .

MACK. (*Having come up beside her through this.*) Jesus!

MABEL. (*Startled.*) Mr. Sennett, you scared me! I didn't know anybody was there.

MACK. Damn right you didn't, what the hell was that, never mind just get one thing straight . . . No star of mine is riding ever-shifting bosoms!

MABEL. (*Laughing.*) It was a poem. I made it up! Well don't look at me as if I just escaped or something . . . didn't you ever make up a poem?

MACK. Me?

MABEL. When you were a kid. Everybody does.

MACK. I don't know, maybe when I was a kid . . .

MABEL. Say it.

MACK. Oh no.

MABEL. Come on, say it.

MACK. Say what, I don't even remember it, it was a hundred years ago, I'm not even sure it was mine, I . . . (*Giving up, a deep breath.*)
Oh God that book that's called the Bible
Which you wrote and I read bits
Says you're good and kind and reliable
So why did you take away poor Fritz.
(*A long silence.* MABEL *just looks at him.*) . . . Well I think it's pretty damn good for a six year old boy! Fritz was my best friend. Half Schnauzer, half German Shepherd which is why I guess God took him. Anyway it's a helluva lot better than Oh, Desert!

MABEL. Of course it is! Then times! You shoulda kept it up.

MACK. Poems? Are you nuts, what've poems got to do with making movies?

MABEL. Does everything have to do with making movies?

MACK. Yes!

MABEL. And what about the other things people are supposed to want. Good times . . . Good friends when you need 'em . . . Good eats when you're hungry . . .

MACK. Luxuries, kid. I can't afford 'em.

MABEL. You might be able to. Like for instance if you found some girl who was friendly, and knew how to have good times, and could cook . . . You'd have it all in one! I don't suppose you're hungry right now, are you?

MACK. What good would it do me, the dining car's closed.

MABEL. Who said anything about dining cars, I got a cooker in my compartment. (*And she takes his hand and leads him Left as Observation Platform goes off and* MABEL's *Compartment comes on.*) . . . Frank and Lottie and me cook in to save money, I have some veal and peppers left over from dinner, I could easily heat it up . . .

MACK. Look, Miss Normand, you're wasting your time! I'm not in the market.

MABEL. (*As she pulls down shade, lights sterno cooker, puts pot on flame.*) Market for what?

MACK. Anything you have in mind! The cook, the good times, the girl . . . I'm not buying.

MABEL. (*Winding up phonograph, putting a wax cylinder on it.*) So who's offering? My God, you cook one lousy veal and peppers like my mother made for my father just before they got married and he thinks he has to make an honest woman out of you . . . (*Putting out silverware.*) Courtsey of the Union Pacific Railroad. Lottie swiped three sets. Down to the napkin rings.

MACK. (*As she passes him plate of veal and peppers.*) I'm

not saying you're not a nice kid, Mabel. You're pretty. Your
veal ain't too bad. And I don't mind spending a little time with
you now and then . . . As long as you understand the rules.
(*And to the accompaniment of the scratchy MUSIC on the
wax cylinder, he sings.*)
I WON'T SEND ROSES
OR HOLD THE DOOR
I WON'T REMEMBER
WHICH DRESS YOU WORE
MY HEART IS TOO MUCH IN CONTROL
THE LACK OF ROMANCE IN MY SOUL
WILL TURN YOU GRAY, KID
SO STAY AWAY, KID
FORGET MY SHOULDER
WHEN YOU'RE IN NEED
FORGETTING BIRTHDAYS
IS GUARANTEED
AND SHOULD I LOVE YOU, YOU WOULD BE
THE LAST TO KNOW
I WON'T SEND ROSES
AND ROSES SUIT YOU SO . . .

(*MUSIC continues as* MACK *reaches over to take her in his
  arms.* MABEL *suddenly pulls back.*)

  MABEL. I forgot about the ring!
  MACK. What ring?
  MABEL. Even if you get married for just one night you still
gotta have a ring. (*She picks up napkin ring.*) . . . I knew it
would come in handy. And it's a good omen! Union, that's
what we're about to do. Pacific. That means peaceful. Go on,
put it on for me.
  MACK. Mabel, this is foolish . . .
  MABEL. Put it on for me, Mack. (*And he reluctantly does.*)
And now you may kiss the bride. (*And* MABEL *moves happily
into his arms as* MACK *continues.*)
  MACK.
MY PACE IS FRANTIC
MY TEMPER'S CROSS
WITH WORDS ROMANTIC
I'M AT A LOSS
I'D BE THE FIRST ONE TO AGREE
THAT I'M PREOCCUPIED WITH ME
AND IT'S IMBRED, KID
SO KEEP YOUR HEAD, KID
IN ME YOU'LL FIND THINGS

LIKE GUTS AND NERVE
BUT NOT THE KIND THINGS
THAT YOU DESERVE
AND SO WHILE THERE'S A FIGHTING CHANCE
JUST TURN AND GO
I WON'T SEND ROSES
AND ROSES SUIT YOU SO.

(The Song ends, phonograph clicks off, LIGHTS fade. In dark Compartment turns so now we see it from exterior. Suddenly there is the sound of train jarring to a stop, window opens, and MACK *sticks his head out.)* Jesus, houses! We're in California! *(And grabbing his clothes he dashes out of the Compartment with a hasty "See ya', kid," paying no attention to* MABEL *who tries to tell him "It's only eight, Mack, we don't get into Los Angeles til nine-fifteen . . ." She calls after him again "Mack?" but he is gone. MUSIC comes up again as* MABEL *leans out the window, looks at early morning as it rolls by in California, and sings.)*

MABEL.
SO WHO NEEDS ROSES
OR STUFF LIKE THAT
SO WHO WANTS CHOCOLATES
THEY'D MAKE ME FAT
AND I CAN GET ALONG JUST FINE
WITHOUT A GUSHING VALENTINE
AND I'LL GET BY, KID
WITH JUST THE GUY, KID
AND IF HE CALLS ME
AND IT'S COLLECT
SIR WALTER RALEIGH
I DON'T EXPECT
AND THOUGH I KNOW I MAY BE LEFT
OUT ON A LIMB
SO WHO NEEDS ROSES
THAT DIDN'T COME FROM HIM.

(Song ends as MABEL *slowly whirls the napkin ring on her finger as LIGHTS fade and we come up on . . .)*

ACT ONE

SCENE 5

Two Flunkies as they start out from Right with a Red Carpet which they fling out to unroll down the length of the Stage as MUSIC of BIG TIME comes up, a "Welcome To Los Angeles" banner flies in and we are in front of Union Station, Los Angeles, 1912. FAMILY *excitedly starts on amid bustle of other Arriving Passengers, Trainmen, etc. A moment of this then* VERY IMPORTANT-LOOKING GENTLE-MAN *followed by* SECRETARY *bearing sheaf of red roses starts on from Left.*

MABEL. (*Entering at same time, seeing roses.*) Mack, you shouldn't have!

MACK. (*To us.*) I didn't. (*And* IMPORTANT-LOOKING GENTLE-MAN *walks past* MABEL *to* MAN *with suitcase who has just come on Right.*)

IMPORTANT GENTLEMAN. . . . Mr. Griffith how good to see you, welcome back to Los Angeles, right this way D.W., the Pierce Arrow's waiting right outside the door . . . (*As they exit.*) By the way Mr. Marvin has asked me to tell you that Ramona has broken box-office records all over the country and it looks like Orphans of the Storm will be the top-grossing feature for 1911 *and* 12 and . . .

KLEIMAN. (*Standing with* Fox *on carpet as Flunkies pull it off.*) Sennett, did you hear that? Pierce Arrow cars you don't get from two-reelers. Now that we're in Hollywood we gotta make epics.

Fox. Forget Beauty and the Buzzsaw, the public wants spectacle!

KLEIMAN. Tragic romance!

Fox. The Fall of Rome!

KLEIMAN. A couple of Gishes freezing in the snow!

MACK. . . . I see what you mean! A Bible story. *Salome!*

KLEIMAN and Fox. (*By now Offstage.*) That's it!

MACK. With Fatty Arbuckle as Salomé and Ben Turpin as John the Baptist! Then we still got those cross-eyes going for us when his head's on the plate. (*As MUSIC comes up.*) It's no use, boys, we ain't cut from the same cloth! Mr. Griffith makes film epics of sweep and grandeur. Mr. Sennett, hell, he just makes movies. (*And he sings.*)

HEARTBREAK AND PASSION
MAY BOTH BE IN FASHION
BUT I WANNA MAKE THE WORLD LAUGH
LET OTHERS DO DRAMA OF SIN AND DISGRACE
WHILE I THROW A FISH IN THE HEROINE'S
  FACE
TO KEEP THEM IN STITCHES
I'D BURN THE STAR'S BRITCHES

AND SAW COUSIN SALLY IN HALF
LET MR. GRIFFITH DEAL WITH HUMANITY'S
    WOES
I'D RATHER FILM THE GUY WITH THE FLY ON
    HIS NOSE
MY GOAL AND MY MISSION
MY BURNING AMBITION
IS . . . I WANNA MAKE THE WORLD LAUGH!

SOME HAVE A LEANING
FOR DARK HIDDEN MEANING
BUT I WANNA MAKE THE WORLD LAUGH
LET OTHER DIRECTOR'S FILM TRAGIC ROMANCE
BUT I LIKE A HERO WITH ANTS IN HIS PANTS
NOTHING I'VE FOUND IS
AS SWEET AS THAT SOUND IS
THE MUSIC THAT FATTENS THE CALF
MY GREAT NEW PLOT IS NOT ABOUT TYRANNY'S
    LASH
IT DEALS WITH ITCHING POWDER AND PAPA'S
    MUSTACHE
THE CURSE I'VE BEEN BLESSED WITH
COMPLETELY POSSESSED WITH
IS . . . I WANNA MAKE THE WORLD LAUGH!
    (*LIGHTS have started down through last of this,* FAMILY
    exits, and at a gesture from MACK *set of Union Station
    disappears and a SCREEN comes down. As MUSIC con-
    tinues, with* MACK *still Onstage, we see on the screen a
    composite of all the early Sennett films, the chases, the
    pies, the pratfalls, the motorcycles crashing through walls,
    the cars driving up stairs, etc., etc. Clip ends with freeze
    shot of motorcycle sailing off cliff, LIGHTS back up on*
    MACK *as he continues.*)
NOTHING I'VE FOUND IS
AS SWEET AS THAT SOUND IS
THE MUSIC THAT FATTENS THE CALF
SO KEEP THE SUDS, THE SCHMALTZ, THE SOAP
    AND THE SOBS
THE ONLY ART I KNOW IS TO TICKLE THE
    SLOBS
THIS CURSE I'VE BEEN BLESSED WITH
COMPLETELY POSSESSED WITH
IS . . . I WANNA MAKE THE WORLD LAUGH!

(*End NUMBER, applause,* MACK *starts to director's chair
    center as we come up on . . .*)

ACT ONE

Scene 6

The New Studio, one year later.

MACK. (*In chair.*) . . . So how did the trouble begin? My damn writer, Frank. He didn't mean to start it, I guess, but that's what he did. Everything was going along fine, I still had my arrangement with Mabel, we were just about to start a new two-reeler . . . God-damn writers, why don't they stick to god-damn playing poker and not write any god-damn scripts!

FRANK. (*Coming on Up Right, reading from script he holds in his hand as* MABEL, *wearing simple dressing gown and carrying lunch in a paper bag, starts in from Left.*) . . . Molly turns! She looks up at Dan. Then she reaches out, takes his hand, and laughs. He laughs with her. The trolley's still waiting, the motorman clangs the bell, are they coming or not? Molly makes up her mind, starts running after the streetcar, Dan right behind her! All the passengers cheer as they jump on board and hand in hand ride off together as the picture ends. (*He closes the manuscript.*) Well, what do you think? And don't be kind, if it's rotten, say so!

MABEL. Rotten? Frank, you must be kidding! It's beautiful! That's the trouble . . .

FRANK. What do you mean?

MABEL. It's too beautiful to waste on me! Frank, Molly's a real person and you need a real actress for the part! Sure, I pass for an actress sometimes but that's because I do what Mack tells me . . . (*Imitating* MACK.) Alright, Miss Normand, count of one you turn, count of two you kick Wally in the behind, count of three Wally kicks you in the behind. That's my kind of acting.

FRANK. (*Crossing to her.*) Mabel, Mabel, don't you even know who you are? Just because that . . . that stultifying despot doesn't know enough to respect your . . .

MABEL. Now, Frank, don't start that again . . . (FRANK *overrides her.*)

FRANK. . . . Your integrity as a artist, doesn't mean that you aren't one of the best actresses on the screen today! I wrote "Molly" for you, Mabel, and nobody *but* you is going to do it!

MABEL. Then it'll never get done. Mack's never let me. And besides everything else, it's a feature film and I only make two-reelers! (FRANK *turns away.*) Hey, you mad?

FRANK. No . . . (*Changing his mind.*) Yes! At you! Because you jump every time that big Irish bum cracks the whip. He's using you, Mabel!

MABEL. Yeah, I know. But I like him, Frank, go fight city hall. (*Putting rest of sandwich in bag.*) . . . I better go or he'll have a fit. (*She starts Right, suddenly stops.*) Hey, Frank, say it again.

FRANK. Say what again?

MABEL. You know. That stuff about integrity.

FRANK. You mean your integrity as an artist.

MABEL. Yeah. Oh, Frank! Ain't baloney beautiful! (*And she hurries Right as* GRIPS *start out with set of ancient Rome,* ACTORS *in togas start to assemble,* MACK *begins setting up camera.*) . . . Alright, Mack, I'm coming!

MACK. Well get a move on, we ain't got all day! Now remember, it's ancient Rome, you're the emperor's new maid, first day on the job, very nervous. Wally, you're the emperor, (*He sashays on in outsize toga.*) Lottie, you're his wife, very dignified, Gertie, Harry, you're some kind of noble Romans or whatever they have. Alright, let's try one. Ella, go! (ELLA *pounds away at some Roman-type MUSIC as* MABEL *crosses to serve the Guests. A moment, then* MACK *interrupts.*) Wait a minute . . . Cut! Mabel, you're not getting there quick enough. You're supposed to trip and spill the soup on Harry *before* he proposes the toast.

MABEL. I know what you want, Mack, but it's hard to walk over there and just spill it. It looks like I'm doing it deliberately.

MACK. Let me worry about what it looks like, you just spill the soup. Look, if it'll help, I'll count.

MABEL. I don't think I need that, Mack.

MACK. It seems to be the only way we get things done! Now let's go from the top. Count of one you get the soup, count of two you turn, count of three four five you walk, count of six you trip and spill the soup. Ella, go! Count of one . . . (MABEL *hasn't moved.*) Cut! What's the matter now?

MABEL. I don't want to do it that way anymore, Mack.

MACK. And why the hell not, may I ask?

MABEL. Because . . . (*She finds the words.*) Because it offends my integrity as an artist!

MACK. Your *what?*

MABEL. (*Weakening.*) My integrity . . . As an artist . . .

MACK. Now I've heard it all! Look, Miss Normand, you make a lot of money, people all over the world know your name, you've got a car, nice clothes, a beautiful home . . .

and you didn't get any of them because you remotely resemble anything you might call an "artist." You got them because *I* counted for you! One you walk, two three you turn, four five six you smile, seven you cry, eight you laugh! Norma Talmadage is an artist, Lillian Gish is an artist, you, Miss Norman, can count up to eight and if I hadn't taught you that you'd still be back in that bean wagon asking for your fifteen cents! Now I am going to count once again and you are going to do what passes for acting. Are you ready? One you turn, two reach for the bowl, three . . . (*And* MABEL *has indeed turned, taken a custard pie from the sideboard, and on three heaves it at* MACK *with all her strength.*)

MABEL. (*As pie splats in his face.*) How's that for four, you . . . (*It comes to her.*) You stultifying despot!

(*A long moment as* MACK *does not move, then slowly he wipes pie from his face, crosses to sideboard, picks up a second pie, carefully aims it and heaves it at* MABEL, *who ducks and runs out as it lands smack in* LOTTIE'S *face. In the ensuing silence we hear* WALLY'S *uncontrollable giggle and as MUSIC comes up,* LOTTIE *takes another pie from sideboard, walks over to* WALLY, *let's fly, and as* WALLY *turns aside pie catches* GRIP *standing behind him. Mayhem spreads, pies fly in earnest,* ELLA *hurries over to stop them and gets two at once. A shout from off and* FOX *comes charging on.*)

FOX. Sennett, what do you think you're doing? We've got a schedule to meet . . . (*Splat,* FOX *gets his. By now almost Everybody is thick with custard as they line up along the apron and sing.*)
ALL.
HEARTBREAK AND PASSION
MAY BOTH BE IN FASHION
BUT WE WANNA MAKE THE WORLD LAUGH
LET OTHERS DO DRAMA OF SIN AND DISGRACE
WHILE WE THROW A PIE IN THE HEROINE'S
    FACE
TO KEEP THEM IN STITCHES
WE BURN THE STAR'S BRITCHES
AND SAW COUSIN SALLY IN HALF
    MACK.
SO KEEP THE SCHMALTZ AND THE SOAP AND
    THE SOBS

ALL.
THE ONLY ART WE KNOW IS TO TICKLE THE
    SLOBS
THIS CURSE WE'VE BEEN BLESSED WITH
COMPLETELY POSSESSED WITH
IS WE WANNA MAKE THE WORLD LAUGH . . .
*(They all start to laugh until one by one, they notice that
    everybody is covered with custard save* WALLY, *who has
    somehow managed to escape unscathed and now laughs
    happily Center alongside* MACK. WALLY's *laughter dies
    away as he becomes aware of the silence of the others.
    Suddenly he turns.)*
    WALLY. See ya', Mack. *(And as he starts Upstage he walks
full into the pie* MACK *has been holding behind his back.
Covered with custard,* WALLY *turns back to line as they all
sing.)*
    ALL.
WE WANNA MAKE THE WORLD LAUGH!

(End NUMBER, applause, BARBER *enters with chair, hands*
    MACK *wet towel as he shouts.)*

    MACK. Andy, Doc, Louie, get this place cleaned up! And
don't forget, we're shooting the chase this afternoon, I want
those trucks loaded and ready to go down to the beach by
two! *(*GRIPS *start cleaning up as* MABEL *comes storming on
Down Right.)*
    MABEL. Mr. Sennett!
    MACK. Yes, Miss Normand!
    MABEL. I'm cooking veal and peppers tonight!
    MACK. I'll be there!
    MABEL. Good! And Mack . . . I'm sorry I hit you with
that pie.
    MACK. I ain't, kid. *(As she exits Right.)* . . . Andy, order
me ten dozen of those pies first thing tomorrow morning. I
gotta helluva idea. *(RAG MUSIC up and First Couple dances
on.* MACK *still in barber chair Down Left.)*
    FRANK. *(Wearing blazer, fancy tie.)* Hey, Mack, better get a
move on, you got that lunch.
    MACK. What lunch?
    FRANK. For Mabel! Screen director's award. Orchid Room
of the Hollywood Hotel. *(Second Couple dances on.)* Just
the sort of "do" you love, boss. Creamed chicken and bananas
on toast points. And an orchestra! Hey, maybe Griffith'll ask
you to dance. *(Both Couples dance as* MABEL, *in tea gown,*

comes dancing on with KLEIMAN. WILLIAM DESMOND TAYLOR *enters at this point, dancing with* PHYLLIS FOSTER.) Okay, Andy, finish it up here, the boss is going to meet the real directors, Griffith, DeMille, Thomas Ince, William Desmond Taylor . . .

MACK. (*As* TAYLOR *leaves* PHYLLIS FOSTER *and cuts in on* MABEL.) William Desmond Taylor. Anyone with half an eye could see that bozo had the word "phony" written all over him! Anyone, that is . . . but Mabel. (*And we are in . . .*)

ACT ONE

SCENE 7

The Orchid Room of the Hollywood Hotel. Columns, potted palms, WAITERS *at stiff-necked attention.*

MABEL. (*As they dance.*) . . . I can't help it, Mr. Taylor, you're just my favorite director in all Hollywood! Do you know how many times I saw "Bondage of Love"? Six! It was wonderful! Especially that scene where Magda the gypsy girl picks up the whip and drives her lover Lord Egbert into the foam-flecked sea! I applauded right there in the theatre! Mr. Taylor, I guess I'm just one of your "adoring fans."

TAYLOR. What a coincidence, so am I. By that I mean I've always been one of your fans, Miss Normand. In fact, I've asked Sennett a dozen times to loan you out for one of my pictures, but he's always turned me down.

MABEL. You wanted me for one of your pictures?

TAYLOR. You sound surprised, didn't Sennett tell you?

MABEL. Oh, you know Mack. He gets busy and forgets. Anyway I've never made anything but two-reelers.

TAYLOR. Exactly why I made the offer. You see, I happen to be one of a large group of people here in Hollywood who think Miss Mabel Normand should have been making feature films a long while ago! In a real studio, not a pie factory.

MACK. (*Muttering from barber chair.*) Sonofabitch . . .

TALYOR. As a matter of fact, it might not be a bad idea if you and I got together and discussed it. I'm giving a little dinner Tuesday and if you're free . . .

MACK. (*He's had enough, from chair.*) She's busy Tuesday. (*A moment, then* MABEL *nods in agreement.*)

MABEL. I'm sorry, I forgot. I'm busy Tuesday.

TAYLOR. Then how about tonight? I know a charming little French restaurant out in Silver Lake . . .

MACK. (*Starting over as* BARBER *exits.*) She's busy tonight, too. We're picking locations for her new movie.

MABEL. Mack, you don't need me for that . . .

MACK. She's busy tonight.

TAYLOR. Some other time, then. (*Handing* MABEL *his card.*) This is my private number if you happen to find a spare moment. I hope it won't be too far in the future. (*Looking at* MACK *as if seeing him for the first time.*) Mack! Good to see you. (*Crossing to him.*) Caught one of your two-reelers the other day. Quite amusing, the entire audience smiled heartily. (*As he exits.*) Good afternoon, Miss Normand. (*And he is gone, followed by* KLEIMAN *and a furious* PHYLLIS FOSTER. MACK *and* MABEL *are alone.*)

MABEL. Why did you do that?

MACK. Do what? Get rid of a phony? You ought to thank me.

MABEL. He's not a phony, Mack. He's a very successful director. And he wants to star me in a feature film.

MACK. Then he's dumber than I thought. The public's not paying good money to see Mabel Normand in more than two reels and without a pie in her face!

MABEL. Mr. Taylor thinks you're wrong, Mack.

MACK. What does that bum know. The old oil, yeah, that he can lay on! I know a charming little French restaurant out in Silver Lake, Miss Normand! And you were lapping it up!

MABEL. Yes, I liked it! It was nice being talked to for a change instead of bellowed at.

MACK. When did I ever bellow?

MABEL. When you breathe! When you tell me how to walk, what to wear, where to go . . . Even when you talk in your sleep!

MACK. God-damn it, I won't have you listening to me when I sleep!

MABEL. (*Softly.*) Then sleep alone. (*And she starts out.*)

MACK. Where do you think you're going? I got cars coming in ten minutes to take us out to the beach for the chase. This is a working day, you know!

MABEL. I'll take a taxi.

MACK. Are you nuts, the cars are paid for!

MABEL. I'll take a taxi!

MACK. Take a damn streetcar if you want but we start shooting at two! With you or without you! Is that clear? (*Suddenly out of scene.*) . . . Stop it, you idiot! Before it's too late, stop it! Apologize, make a joke, what the hell, take her in your arms! Sure it didn't happen but what's an artist for if he can't change life! (*A moment, then with great effort he turns back to scene.*) With you or without you! Is that clear?

MABEL. (*A shout, as he goes.*) Yes, Mr. Sennett! It's perfectly clear! (*And she sings.*)

THIS NINNY OF A PUPPET WAS AVAILABLE THE
      SECOND THAT HE CALLED!
AND ALL HE HAD TO DO WAS YELL "HEY,
      MABEL" AND THIS DUMB HASH-SLINGER
      CRAWLED!
FOR SEVEN LOUSY YEARS I'VE WATCHED HIM
      SWEAR AND SHOVE AND SHOUT
"WITH YOU OR WITHOUT YOU!"
WELL IT'S GONNA BE WITHOUT.

I GOTTA GIVE MY LIFE SOME SPARKLE AND
      FIZZ
AND THINK A THOUGHT THAT ISN'T WRAPPED
      UP IN HIS
THE PLACE THAT I CONSIDER PARADISE IS
WHEREVER HE AIN'T! WHEREVER HE AIN'T!

NO MORE TO WITHER WHEN HE'S GROUCHY
      AND GRUFF
NO MORE TO LISTEN TO HIM BELLOW AND
      BLUFF
TOMORROW MORNING I'LL BE STRUTTIN' MY
      STUFF
WHEREVER HE AIN'T! WHEREVER HE AIN'T!

ENOUGH OF BEING BULLIED AND BOSSED
TA-TA, AUF WIEDERSEHEN, AND GET LOST!

I WALKED BEHIND HIM LIKE A MEEK LITTLE
      LAMB
AND HAD MY FILL OF HIS NOT GIVIN' A DAMN
I'LL GO TO SYDNEY OR CEYLON OR SIAM
WHEREVER HE AIN'T! WHEREVER HE AIN'T!

(WAITERS *have come back to clear tables, get carried away by* MABEL's *rebellion and join her as she dances. Dance interlude ends with* MABEL *up on table being pushed around by* WAITERS *as she sings.*)

IT'S TIME FOR LITTLE NELL TO REBEL
IF HE'S IN HEAVEN, I'LL GO TO HELL!

MY LITTLE LOVE NEST WAS A TERRIBLE TRAP
WITH ME BEHAVING LIKE A SIMPERING SAP
AND SO I'M LOOKING FOR A SPOT ON THE MAP
IF HE'S GOIN' SOUTH
I'M GOIN' NORTH
IF HE'S GOIN' BACK
I'M GOIN' FORTH
WHEREVER HE AIN'T!

(*And* MABEL *and* WAITERS *exit Left as we come up on . . .*)

ACT ONE

SCENE 8

The Studio Gate as GRIPS *start out carrying trunks, reflectors,*
cameras, etc.

ANDY. . . . Come on, come on, the trucks are waiting, get
this stuff loaded! And watch it, huh, I don't want nothing
busted when we get to the beach. Easy with that camera, Doc!
Look, maybe you better put it in front with me. (MABEL
strides on through this, marches Down Right.) Miss Normand,
where you been? Boss says we gotta leave two sharp!

MABEL. (*Taking suitcase from* WARDROBE LADY, *who has*
entered Down Right, looking hastily through it.) . . . Iris, my
tin box. Where is it?

IRIS. It should be there, Miss Normand, I packed it this
morning.

MABEL. Maybe it's up in wardrobe, look for it, Iris, will you?
I don't need the box, just something that's in it . . . A damn
napkin ring! But it's the one think in this place that's mine
and I want it! (MACK *coming on as* IRIS *starts off, saying.*)

IRIS. Yes, Miss Normand, I'll look for it right away.

MACK. . . . Alright, let's get started. Lottie, you're in the
first car with Ella, Wally with Frank and me, come on, get
a move on . . . (MABEL *starts past him.*) Well it's damn about
time, go on, you're in the first car with Lottie and Ella, hey
where do you think you're going?

MABEL. To dinner!

MACK. At two in the afternoon?

MABEL. Yes, Mr. Sennett! It's a long drive out to Silver
Lake.

MACK. Oh I see, I see, so that's it, that "charming little
French restaurant." . . . Well, go on, go! We'll just cut your
part out of the chase, it was slowing things down, anyway.

LOTTIE. Hey, Mack, take it easy . . .

MACK. Easy's just how I'm taking it, Lottie! Miss Normand's going to be an "artist" now and I say that's just dandy! Go on, make a six-reeler, make a ten-reeler, make a hundred reeler! Let the audience bring their beds to the movie house so they can watch you play your god-damn gypsies with their god-damn whips driving your god-damn English lords . . .

MABEL. (*Exiting.*) Goodbye, Mack.

MACK. Into the god-damn foam-flecked sea! (*And she is gone. A moment of stunned silence, then a furious* LOTTIE *crosses to* MACK.)

LOTTIE. Mack, do you know what you are . . .

WALLY. Geez, Mack, did you have to say them things?

LOTTIE. A horse's behind!

FRANK. Had to make that rotten speech, didn't you!

LOTTIE. A grade-A number one . . .

ELLA. Honest, Mack, sometimes you just ain't got no sense!

LOTTIE. Horse's butt!

KLEIMAN. (*Hurrying on.*) Sennett, what's wrong? Mabel just walked out the gate!

FOX. She's supposed to go to the beach for the chase, what's going on?

FRANK. Another brilliant Sennett touch, he just let Mabel go!

KLEIMAN. Are you crazy, are you nuts, who's gonna star in all our pictures?

LOTTIE. Don't answer, big shot! But take it from me this studio's gonna miss Mabel a helluva lot more than you think!

MACK. (*Quietly.*) . . . Wrong! This studio's still got Sennett and that's all it ever needed.

FOX. And who's gonna be up there on that screen?

MACK. Other Mabels! I made one out of a hash slinger, what's to stop me from making another? Give me two weeks, Mr. Kleiman, and you'll have more Mabels than you know what to do with!

KLEIMAN. We ain't got two weeks, Sennett! We got a schedule!

MACK. Then I'll find one now! In two minutes! Here! At the beach! (*MUSIC swirls up as* FAMILY *goes off, Hot Dog Vendor with gaily colored cart starts on, and we are at Santa Monica Beach.*) . . . Hell, the sand's full of 'em! (*First Bathing Beauty starts on with beach ball, followed by Second and Third with skiprope and parasol, as* MACK *sings.*)

I'LL MAKE A STAR AND A HALF OUT OF THAT ONE

THE ONE WITH THE DIMPLES, THE REDHEAD,
   THE FAT ONE
HOW 'BOUT THE ONE ON THE BLANKET, THE
   ONE PLAYING BALL
LET'S TAKE 'EM BOTH . . . AH TO HELL WITH
   IT . . .
LET'S TAKE 'EM ALL!

WHAT GIVES A MAN
GINGER AND SNAP
GOIN' THROUGH LIFE
WITH HIS LITTLE OL' LAP
FULL OF HUNDREDS AND HUNDREDS OF GIRLS

WHAT GIVES A MAN
POWER AND PUNCH
TINA FOR BREAKFAST
AND LENA FOR LUNCH
HAVING HUNDREDS AND HUNDREDS OF GIRLS
SHOW HIM A BLONDE
AND SOMETHING IN HIS SOUL WILL LEAP TO
   RESPOND
BUT THEN AGAIN HE'S ALSO TERRIBLY FOND
OF THIS BRUNETTE AND SO
INSTEAD OF ONE DANDY DISH
PASS HIM THE CANDY DISH

I'LL SPRINKLE SPICE
INTO HIS LIFE
TO MAKE HIM FORGET
THAT HE'S STUCK WITH HIS WIFE
GIVE HIM HUNDREDS AND HUNDREDS OF
   GIRLS!

BEULAH AND BELLE
GLADYS AND GERT
TWO FOR THE ENTREE
AND THREE FOR DESSERT
GIVE 'EM HUNDREDS AND HUNDREDS OF GIRLS

FOUR ON A SLIDE
FIVE ON A SWING
I'M GONNA MAKE
THE CASH REGISTER RING
HAVING HUNDREDS AND HUNDREDS OF GIRLS

I'LL FILL THE SCREEN
WITH JAN AND JANE AND JOAN AND JANET
      AND JEAN
I'LL PULL THE GREATEST STUNT THIS BUSINESS
      HAS SEEN
TIL EV'RY FELLA FROM DULUTH TO ATLANTA
      SEES
ALL OF HIS FANTASIES!
LOOK!

(*And as* MACK *points,* GIRLS *slide one by one down a giant
slide that has come in through above. As each Bathing
Beauty comes down, she joins the line that stretches across
the apron as they sing.*)

   GIRLS.
WHAT GIVES A MAN
GINGER AND SNAP
GOIN' THROUGH LIFE
WITH HIS LITTLE OL' LAP
FULL OF HUNDREDS AND HUNDREDS OF GIRLS

WHAT GIVES A MAN
POWER AND PUNCH
TINA FOR BREAKFAST
AND LENA FOR LUNCH
HAVING HUNDREDS AND HUNDREDS OF GIRLS
   MACK.
ANALYSTS FIND
THIS THING CALLED MODERN MAN WAS NEVER
      DESIGNED
WITH ONLY ONE ETERNAL PARTNER IN MIND
AND SO I GOTTA YELL TO HELL WITH
      PROPRIETY
VIVA VARIETY

SINNER OR SAINT
SCHOOLGIRL OR QUEEN
ONE GIRL IS BORING
AND TWO ARE OBSCENE
GIVE 'EM HUNDREDS AND HUNDREDS OF GIRLS!
(*NUMBER becomes a dance with* MACK, *the* GIRLS, *and
occasionally* WALLY *in an outsized bathing suit of the period,
then builds to climax as* ANDY *brings out the camera and* MACK
films them in typical Bathing Beauty poses.)
   MACK. Alright, girls, you're at the seashore and having a

wonderful time! Here comes the water, now get those tootsies
in. Ooh, it's cold! Now the other tootsie! Now both tootsies
and into the waves! Now the waves get higher and higher,
and higher . . .
(GIRLS *form a line and come kicking down to the edge of the
        Stage, each one in a different Bathing Beauty pose. One
        final shot by* MACK *and the NUMBER ends. Applause,*
        KLEIMAN, FOX, *and* WALLY *rush out to congratulate*
        MACK.)

KLEIMAN. (*Waving newspaper.*) Front page of the New
York *World!* Mack Sennett and his Bathing Beauties!
    FOX. More pictures on pages two, three, and four!
    KLEIMAN. Text of President Wilson's speech to Congress,
page twenty-two. You've done it, Sennett! We couldn't get
publicity like this for a million bucks! (MACK *moves Down
Right as MUSIC comes up and* GIRLS *move into several
groups of typical Bathing Beauty shots. MUSIC out and they
freeze.*)
    KLEIMAN. We're in clover, Sennett! That Bathing Beauty
publicity's boosted the gross in the last six two-reelers nearly
fifty percent!
    FOX. Every magazine in the country wants some shots, I
even got a call from the *National Geographic!* (*MUSIC up
again, there are fewer* GIRLS *now, another set of poses.*)
    FOX. (*As MUSIC goes out,* GIRLS *freeze.*) A house record
in Cincinnati, Sennett, sixty thousand bucks!
    KLEIMAN. New York just called, Mack. They gotta have
more, and more . . . (*MUSIC up, the remaining* GIRLS *dance
off,* WALLY *slowly off after last* GIRL. *Lights have gone to half.*
MACK *is alone, MUSIC comes softly up as he sings.*)
    MACK.
FORGET MY SHOULDER
WHEN YOU'RE IN NEED
FORGETTING BIRTHDAYS
IS GUARANTEED
AND SHOULD I LOVE YOU, YOU WOULD BE
THE LAST TO KNOW
I WON'T SEND ROSES
AND ROSES SUIT YOU SO.

(*The MUSIC finishes out the phrase as lights pinpoint* MACK
        . . . *and the battered napkin ring . . . as he throws it,
        catches it, throws it, catches it, then walks slowly Upstage
        and CURTAIN comes down on.*)

END OF ACT ONE

ACT TWO

SCENE 1

ENTRE-ACTE does not finish but segues to SCREEN [See Note Bottom Page] and shot of MABEL, *handsomely dressed, standing atop elegant staircase. Her look is tense, she breathes rapidly. Camera pulls back to reveal* WILLIAM DESMOND TAYLOR *in evening clothes beside her.* MABEL *turns to him and we cut to Title No. 1:* "There is no other way, Nigel. I want a divorce!" *Framing of title says* Woman Of Scandal *on top and* A William Desmond Taylor Production *on bottom. Cut to shot of* TAYLOR *laughing sardonically then Title No. 2:* "Never, Cynthia! These marriage chains will bind you to me forever!" *Shot of* MABEL *whirling on him, eyes flashing, lips moving in a soundless sentence. Title No. 3:* "How I hate you, hate you, hate you!" *Cut to* TAYLOR *as he raises his hand to strike her.* MABEL *recoils, Title No. 4:* "You would strike a woman, wouldn't you!" *Cut to* MABEL *as she scornfully flings her fur wrap around her shoulders and starts down stairs. SCREEN suddenly goes blank as we hear a shout* . . .

MACK. . . . Kill it! Kill it, it's lousy! (*Coming on, followed by* FRANK.) That sonofabitch Taylor is ruining her! Did you see those clothes? Who does he think she is, Tashman? It's Mabel, the girl-next-door, everybody's pal!

FRANK. Glad to hear you say that, Mack, cause I've got an idea.

*MACK. . . . Sure I walked out! Worst God-damn movie I ever saw. That sonofabitch Taylor is ruining her! Five lousy pictures in five years! When's Mabel gonna wise up and quit that bum?

FRANK. Same question I've been asking myself, boss, and as a matter of fact I've got a little idea.

MACK. (*Having peeled off his jacket, now removing tie and shirt as* MACK's *New Office starts in around them.*) We got a story conference tomorrow at three, save it til then.

*Note: If film is an impossibility we segue directly from ENTRE-ACTE to MACK'S OFFICE as he takes off coat, throws it to FRANK who follows him.

FRANK. Ask her back.

MACK. What?

FRANK. Mabel. Ask her back.

MACK. You used to deliver papers, what'd you do forget how to read 'em? (*Picking up newspaper from his desk.*) "Miss Mabel Normand sailing to Paris with director William Desmond Taylor to research backgrounds for her next picture." What do you want me to do, drag 'er off the boat?

FRANK. She's not leaving til the end of the month. One call from you and that trip'd be off.

MACK. (*Now down to pants and undershirt, crossing behind screen Up Left.*) Anyhow what the hell do I need Mabel for? I got the Bathing Beauties!

FRANK. You've had 'em for five years, Mack. It's 1923. The public wants more than a line of giggling girls. Get Mabel back!

MACK. I told you yesterday, Frank, the answer is no. (*By now* GRIPS *have removed screen to reveal* MACK *in huge bathtub in the middle of his office. Hat still on his head as* KLEIMAN *comes in and we see this is the conference* MACK *spoke of.*)

KLEIMAN. . . . It's the grosses, Sennett! Sure we're still making money, but less than two years ago. And two years ago was less than two years before that.

FOX. (*Joining him.*) And that was the year Mabel left!

MACK. And where are the Bathing Beauties?

FOX. Still on Page One.

MACK. And President Coolidge?

KLEIMAN. Page Seventeen. But he's moving up!

MACK. No Mabel! (WALLY *comes on holding script.*)

WALLY. . . . Hey, Mack, this airplane picture is a great idea but it won't work without the right one to play opposite me! Gotta be small, with big round eyes, a cupid's bow mouth and an adorable little figure.

MACK. (*To* FOX, *standing alongside tub.*) Good news, Fox, you're gonna be in pictures. (LOTTIE *and* ELLA *have come on through this,* LOTTIE *pushes aside screen and looks into tub.*)

LOTTIE. You're right, Ella, he has got three. (*Then angrily.*) Mack, I once called you a horse's behind but flattery got me nowhere! Now look, you dim-witted loud-mouthed Irish bonehead . . . Get Mabel back!

MACK. (*To us.*) And that way when I got another one of my great ideas! I decided to ask Mabel back. And I agreed that if she called me up personally, or begged in writing, or maybe got down on her knees in front of the whole studio, I might even let her do that damn script Frank wrote for her. Mabel's reaction was not the same as mine. She didn't have my 'largesse' of spirit. They just told her that Mack needed her. And of course she came. (*A shout as* GRIPS *start hauling him off still in bathtub, as others hastily exit.*) . . . Well what are you waiting for? Get the hell outa here! We got a six-thirty call! Move!

(*The Office is struck, the Stage cleared. LIGHTS start down through this and MUSIC comes softly up as we find our-selves in . . .*)

ACT TWO

SCENE 2

The Studio, early next morning. At first there is nothing but silence then as first faint morning LIGHT begins to come up we see a figure starting down the studio street. The figure approaches, opens the door, then tentatively steps into the empty Studio. It is MABEL. *She wears a plain dark coat, carries a paper bag. She walks across the room, smiles as she touches that old stuffed horse from the movie she made for* MACK *so long ago, finally sits on platform of camera crane Down Center, opens the paper bag and takes out thermos of coffee and a doughnut. She's just about to pour it when* WATCHMAN *comes on.*

WATCHMAN. (*Startled.*) . . . Miss Normand! What are you doing here? It's six in the morning!

MABEL. Hi, Eddie. Oh I just wanted to be here early. Get the feel of the place again.

WATCHMAN. The crew doesn't even get here til half-past! And they got a whole welcome for you! I better call some-body . . .

MABEL. Ah, let 'em sleep. Come on, have some coffee. (*He hesitates, she makes room for him on the platform.*) Come on. (*Doesn't know what to do, still mutters "I really oughta call somebody . . ."* MABEL *pats the platform.*) Come on! (*And he finally sits.*) . . . You like doughnuts?

WATCHMAN. (*Taking half a doughnut she hands him.*) I'm crazy about 'em.

MABEL. (*She pours him coffee from thermos.*) Go on, Eddie. Dunk.

WATCHMAN. Aah, what the hell! (*And he gaily dunks. Then suddenly bursting out.*) . . . Oh, Mabel, you don't know how we've missed you!

MABEL. Now cut it out, Eddie, or I swear I'm gonna bust out cryin' and it'll be your fault!

WATCHMAN. I can't help it, Mabel! (*And he sings.*)
SOMEHOW THE CEILING
SEEMS A LITTLE HIGHER
FROM THE VERY MOMENT I SEE MABEL COME
    IN THE ROOM
IT FEELS LIKE SOMEONE
LIT A ROARING FIRE
BUT IT'S JUST THE GLOW I GET WHEN MABEL
    COMES IN THE ROOM
THE FADED SOFA
STANDS A LITTLE PROUDER
THAT BUNCH OF ARTIFICIAL FLOWERS MIGHT
    EVEN BLOOM
I CAN FEEL MY HEARTBEAT
BEAT A LITTLE LOUDER
THE VERY MOMENT I SEE MABEL COME IN THE
    ROOM.

(*Somewhere through this* MABEL *has moved up onto seat of crane and now as* GRIPS *come on [wearing coats, lumberjackets, etc., they have just come to work] they release crane and send* MABEL *high into the air above them as they sing.*)

GRIPS.
THE DINGY CURTAINS
SEEM A LITTLE BRIGHTER
I CAN HEAR THE TINNY PIANO PLAYIN' A
    GORGEOUS SONG
THE GROUCHY DOORMAN
SEEMS A BIT POLITER
IT'S HIS WAY OF SAYING "WELCOME HOME,
    YOU'VE BEEN GONE TOO LONG"
WATCHMAN.
THE DAY YOU LEFT US
WAS A SMALL DISASTER
YOU TOOK THE LOVE AND LIGHT AND
    LAUGHTER AND LEFT THE GLOOM
WATCHMAN and GRIPS. (*By now* MABEL *is sailing out above the audience.*)

BUT I CAN FEEL MY HEARTBEAT
BEAT A LITTLE FASTER
AND I CAN SWIFTLY SHED THE STRAIN OF THE
 YEARS
THE VERY MOMENT HER FIRST FOOTSTEP
 APPEARS
(*Crane swings down,* MABEL *hops off into their arms as*
 WATCHMAN *sings.*)
 WATCHMAN.
THE VERY MOMENT I SEE MABEL COME IN THE
 ROOM.

(WALLY *has come on through last of this, now sheds his coat*
 and sneaks up behind MABEL. *As MUSIC continues he*
 puts his hands over her eyes and they do peek-a-boo dance
 until she finally sees him and he swings her around to be
 caught by FRANK *who has entered Left.* FRANK *and*
 MABEL, *and then* WALLY, *do a soft shoe and are joined*
 by KLEIMAN *and* FOX *who hurry in with a large banner*
 saying "Welcome Mabel." They fold MABEL *up in it and*
 join the dance as ELLA, *pushed by* TWO GRIPS, *pounding*
 away at the piano comes rolling in.)

 ELLA and GRIPS.
THE THREADBARE CARPET
SEEMS A LITTLE THICKER
FROM THE VERY MOMENT I SEE MABEL COME
 THROUGH THE DOOR
 ALL GRIPS.
THE ELEVATOR
RUNS A LITTLE QUICKER
JUST AS IF IT DIDN'T WANT TO STOP AT
 ANOTHER FLOOR
 LOTTIE. (*Rushing on, arms outstretched.*)
THE KIDS FROM KEYSTONE
ARE THE KIDS NO LONGER
WE MISS JUST HAVING YOU AROUND AND THE
 OLD RAPPORT
 ALL plus GRIPS.
BUT I CAN FEEL MY HEARTBEAT
BEAT A LITTLE STRONGER
AND I CAN SWIFTLY SHED THE STRAIN OF THE
 YEARS

THE VERY MOMENT HER FIRST FOOTSTEP
    APPEARS
THE VERY MOMENT I SEE . . .

    BATHING BEAUTIES. (*In street clothes, having just come to work, a happy shout.*) MABEL!

(GIRLS *and* GRIPS *sing LA-LA CHORUS as* MABEL *is swept up by* FAMILY *into dance. Dance continues as* ALL *sing.*)

    ALL.
THE FADED SOFA
STANDS A LITTLE PROUDER
THAT BUNCH OF ARTIFICIAL FLOWERS MIGHT
    EVEN BLOOM!
BLOOM!
I CAN FEEL MY HEARTBEAT
BEAT A LITTLE LOUDER
AND I CAN SWIFTLY SHED THE STRAIN OF THE
    YEARS
THE VERY MOMENT HER FIRST FOOTSTEP
    APPEARS
THE VERY MOMENT I SEE MABEL COME IN . . .
    (*Dance has built to climax as* ALL *sing.*)
THE ROOM!

(*End NUMBER, applause, in the midst of which* MACK *comes on. As each member of the crowd sees him he or she falls silent. The silence is complete as* MACK *finally stands face to face with* MABEL. *He looks at her for a long moment, then sings.*)

    MACK. (*With all the tenderness he has held back for so long.*)
SOMEHOW THE CEILING
SEEMS A LITTLE HIGHER
FROM THE VERY MOMENT I SEE MABEL COME
    IN THE ROOM
IT FEELS LIKE SOMEONE
LIT A ROARING FIRE
BUT IT'S JUST THE GLOW I GET WHEN MABEL
    COMES IN THE ROOM
    (*MUSIC continues as* MACK *takes* MABEL *in his arms and they dance. He is still holding her as he continues.*)
I CAN FEEL MY HEARTBEAT
BEAT A LITTLE LOUDER

(*MUSIC fades.*) . . . That's what I should have said. That's what I *wanted* to say! But that's not what came out. (*Putting out his arms.*) Kid!

MABEL. Mack!

MACK. Hey, you look like a million!

MABEL. Hey, so do you!

MACK. But we can go into all that later, the big thing now is you're back, so let's get to work. We're gonna do Frank's script like a promised . . . Only with a few Sennett touches.

FRANK. Touches?

MACK. To flesh things out! Now I'm not changing your script, Frank, just giving it some bounce. Like in the first scene on the park bench where Dan tells Molly he loves her, we shoot it *as is!* Only sitting next to them is a gorilla.

FRANK. That'll give it some bounce alright. Hey, Mack, I got another Sennett touch, why bother with Dan at all, let the gorilla tell Molly he loves her . . .

LOTTIE. Then hand in tail they lope off into the sunset!

MACK. (*Disgustedly.*) Alright, alright, cut the gorilla! I was just trying to pep things up but if everybody's going to make such a damn fuss we'll do the damn script the way it is!

MABEL. (*Taking his hand.*) Thank you, Mack. (*Taking off her coat.*) . . . Alright, boss, when do we start?

MACK. When do you think? Now! This is a Sennett production, we can't afford to sit around! Andy, Doc, Louie, set up the park scene! The rest of you get the hell outa here and into costume, I'm shooting in ten minutes! (*As Actors hurry off,* GRIPS *start on with park bench.*) Ah, kid we're gonna make Molly the best feature ever filmed. Hell, how can we miss? We got Sennett and Normand back together again! And there ain't no monkey on earth can top that. (*Two* KOPS *have wandered on through this,* MACK *notices them.*) Not yet, boys, I'll call you when you come on.

MABEL. (*Looking after them as they exit.*) Mack, what was that?

MACK. Nothing, a couple of cops, local color for the park.

MABEL. I don't remember any cops in Frank's script.

MACK. There aren't! It's just background. Couple of crazy policemen we beat up now and then, nothing the public likes more. But I don't let it get out of hand! Two cops that's all. Three at the most. And I only use 'em when I have to, five, six, seven times a reel. And you're right in there with them all the time! Watching.

MABEL. Mack, Molly's the lead, she shouldn't be just watching.

MACK. Right, she shouldn't be just watching. I'll give you a book to read! The Bible.

MABEL. (*Beginning to get annoyed.*) Wonderful, maybe you can count for me while I read, one I finish the Old Testament, two I start on the New Testament . . .

MACK. Hey, hey, trust Sennett kid, don't he always know what's best? Now I tell you what, why don't you wait in your dressing room while I shoot a few seconds of cop background without you, and I'll call you as soon as the real scene begins.

MABEL. You're sure it's just background?

MACK. Just background.

MABEL. Way, way down there in the back?

MACK. Way, way, *way* down there in the back.

MABEL. Alright, Mack, I'll be waiting.

MACK. (*As she starts off.*) That's my girl!

MABEL. In my dressing room.

MACK. While I shoot a few little seconds of one or two tiny cops . . .

MABEL. (*Finishing sentence with him.*) Way, way, *way* down there in the back. (*And with a grunted "Mmm yeah" she exits.* MACK *immediately turns Left.*)

MACK. (*As they come wheeling out Right and Left.*) Mr. Kleiman! Mr. Fox! Good news, I'm shooting some extra background stuff for Molly.

FOX. What's so good about that?

KLEIMAN. It's costing a mint already!

MACK. Which ain't nothing compared to the mint it's gonna make! Now I'll need a couple of cops. And a paddy wagon. Make that three cops and two paddy wagons. And a station-house I can blow up, we'll need some cops in there. Plus a Sergeant and a Chief, that's six, seven, eight . . . Oh hell, make it a whole squad! (*As MUSIC comes up and* MACK *gets more and more carried away.*) . . . We'll call them The Kops. Mack's Kops. Alright, the Keystone Kops! And we'll knock 'em down, flatten 'em under steam rollers, shove 'em over cliffs, poor suffering bastards we'll murder them! Give the public a good healthy dose of brutality, Mr. Kleiman . . .

KLEIMAN. It'll make 'em hate us!

MACK. Yeah, but it'll make us rich! (*At last they see the light as* MACK *sings.*)

HIT 'EM ON THE HEAD

KLEIMAN and FOX.

HA HA HA

MACK.

KICK 'EM IN THE SHINS

KLEIMAN and Fox.
HA HA HA
    MACK.
THE HEROINE'S BEHIND
IS OH SO RIPE FOR BRUISING
LASH 'EM IN THE LOIN
    KLEIMAN and Fox.
HA HA HA
    MACK.
GRIND 'EM IN THE GROIN
    KLEIMAN and Fox.
HA HA HA
    MACK.
AUDIENCE' FIND
THAT PAIN IS SO AMUSING
EVERYBODY LOVES A LITTLE RABBIT PUNCHING
EVERYBODY LOVES THE SOUND OF KNUCKLES
    CRUNCHING
SO FLATTEN SOMEONE'S NOSE
    KLEIMAN and Fox.
HA HA HA
    MACK.
STUB SOMEBODY'S TOES
    KLEIMAN and Fox.
HA HA HA
    MACK.
MAKE A LITTLE THUD
DRAW A LITTLE BLOOD
HIT 'EM ON THE HEAD!
    KLEIMAN and Fox.
HA HA HA

    (Cut-out of Stationhouse starts in through following.)
    MACK.
MASH 'EM IN THE MOUTH
    KLEIMAN and Fox.
HA HA HA
    MACK.
JAB 'EM IN THE JAW
    KLEIMAN and Fox.
HA HA HA
    MACK.
GIVE A VIOLENT SHOVE, AND MAKE IT
    REALISTIC

CLUB 'EM ON THE HIP
   KLEIMAN and Fox.
HO HO HO
   MACK.
MAKE A SWOLLEN LIP
   KLEIMAN and Fox.
HO HO HO
   MACK.
AUDIENCES LOVE TO BE A BIT SADISTIC
   ALL THREE.
PEOPLE JUST ADORE A FIGHT THAT'S DEATH
   DEFYING
LOVE IT EVEN MORE WHEN THERE ARE
   BULLETS FLYING
   KLEIMAN and Fox.
SO, THRASH 'EM IN THE THIGH,
   MACK.
HA HA HA
   KLEIMAN and Fox.
BLACKEN SOMEONE'S EYE
   MACK.
HA HA HA
   KLEIMAN and Fox.
GET 'EM IN THE GUT
   MACK.
BRUISE 'EM ON THE BUTT
   ALL THREE.
HIT 'EM ON THE HEAD!

CAUSE A LITTLE WRECK, HA HA HA
BREAK SOMEBODY'S NECK, HA HA HA
SHOOT A LITTLE GUN, YES, FOLKS IT'S
   SCINTILLATING,
WATCH THE FELLA REEL AND SLIP ON THAT
   BANANA PEEL, HA HA
THE PUBLIC FINDS IT FUN WHEN IT'S
   EXCRUCIATING
EVERYBODY LOVES TO SEE POLICEMAN FUTILE
   IN BREAKING UP A BRAWL
THAT'S BEEN DIVINELY BRUTAL,
SO, BITE 'EM IN THE CALF, HA HA HA
LISTEN TO 'EM LAUGH, HA HA HA , MAKE A
   LITTLE SLASH,
MAKE A WIDER GASH, HIT 'EM ON THE HEAD
   (*Stage biz.*)

MALE CHORUS.
EVERYBODY LOVES TO SEE POLICEMAN FUTILE
    IN
BREAKING UP A BRAWL THAT'S BEEN DIVINELY
    BRUTAL, SO
HIT 'EM ON THE HEAD HA HA HA, KICK 'EM
    ON THE SHINS, HA HA HA

MACK.	CHORUS.
MAKE A LITTLE THUD	DRAW A LITTLE BLOOD
GET 'EM IN THE GUT	BASTE 'EM ON THE BUTT
MAKE A LITTLE SLASH	MAKE A WIDER GASH

ALL.
HIT 'EM ON THE HEAD.
    MACK and KOPS.
EVERYBODY LOVES TO SEE POLICEMAN FUTILE
BREAKING UP A BRAWL THAT'S BEEN DIVINELY
    BRUTAL, SO
BITE 'EM ON THE CALF HA HA HA,
    LISTEN TO 'EM LAUGH HA HA HA
MAKE A LITTLE SLASH, MAKE A WIDER GASH
HIT 'EM ON THE HEAD

(End NUMBER, applause, KLEIMAN and FOX come hurrying
    on as KOPS, except for WALLY, start out by ones and
    twos through following.)

KLEIMAN. . . . Another call from an exhibitor, Sennett!
The Kops In The Park is the best two-reeler you ever made!
    FOX. It's the same all over the country! Atlanta, Cleveland,
Seattle, Des Moines, they want Kops and more Kops!
    MACK. Mr. Kleiman, did you reach Mabel?
    KLEIMAN. I tried again this morning, Mack. She was gone.
    MACK. Well leave a message. Tell her I finish The Kops In
The Pie Factory tomorrow . . . that makes four of them in
the can . . . and we'll be ready to start Molly first thing next
week!
    FRANK. (Coming on through last of this.) He means gone,
Mack. Three weeks is a long time to wait in a dressing room.
    MACK. What the hell are you talking about! Gone where?
    FRANK. That trip to Paris. She took the train East this
morning. Said to tell you she enjoyed reading the Bible and
was glad it ended happy.
    WALLY. (Gently.) Mack, maybe we went too far with them
cops.
    MACK. (Passionately.) How could I help myself, Wally!

Sure, Molly's a helluva script but it ain't never gonna make people laugh and that's what Sennett's all about! And my two-reelers can make 'em laugh wherever in this world they got cops and that's from here to Timbuktu! Think of it, Frank! People I don't know, talking some language I never even heard of, looking up at a bedsheet strung between two trees and laughing because of me! (*Out front.*) I couldn't let it get away, Mabel! I couldn't let it get away! (*He is interrupted by the sound of a boat horn. LIGHTS start to go down,* WALLY, KLEIMAN, FOX *back slowly Off Right and Left.*) Frank . . .

FRANK. Yeah, boss.

MACK. When does that damn boat leave?

FRANK. Next Tuesday, Mack.

MACK. (*As* FRANK *exits, now alone.*) Next Tuesday.

(*Horn blasts again, MUSIC comes up, gangway starts in and we find ourselves on . . .*)

ACT TWO

SCENE 3

Pier 88, New York, eleven-thirty that Tuesday evening. MACK *takes a belted coat that is handed to him by Dockhands as they start on with trunks, suitcases, etc. MUSIC has come up through this and as* MACK *exits,* TAYLOR, PHYLLIS FOSTER, *two other couples dance on. It is a twenties sailing party, hip flasks, Charlestons. MUSIC continues as* MABEL *starts down gangway through dance.*

MABEL. Bill, I . . . (*As she sees* TAYLOR *and* PHYLLIS *dancing together.*) Bill, I looked everywhere, I can't find it.

TAYLOR. Find what, darling?

MABEL. My red suitcase. I saw everything else go on . . .

TAYLOR. (*Leaving* PHYLLIS, *patiently as if to a child.*) Darling, why do you think we're traveling with a secretary? (*Putting his arm around shoulder of* YOUNG MAN *who is with one of the other girls.*) Serge worries about suitcases, we enjoy ourselves. Or try to. Now where was I? (*Turning back to* PHYLLIS.) Oh yes. (*Dance continues as* MABEL *begins looking among suitcases on dock. Dance ends with* PHYLLIS *and* TAYLOR *in an embrace.*)

MABEL. (*As MUSIC continues.*) Bill, my God, if you keep that up they'll never let us on the boat.

TAYLOR. The French Line? They'll give us our passage free. (*Releasing* PHYLLIS.) However if it offends your delicate sensibilities, Miss Normand, we can continue this touching scene in the privacy of our stateroom. (*To others.*) Main deck, children. Forty-four and forty six. (*As others start dancing up gangway.*) . . . Aren't you coming, darling?

MABEL. In a minute, Bill.

TAYLOR. (*Wearily.*) The red suitcase.

MABEL. I'll feel better if I see it go on, it's got all my shoes, my gloves . . .

TAYLOR. (*With a sigh as he exits after others.*) It's like traveling with your maiden aunt. (*And he is gone.*)

(MABEL *turns to talk to* PURSER *as* MACK *enters far up Left. He wears coat, carries a long white flower box.* MABEL *does not see him. He looks at her a moment, then makes up his mind and starts briskly past her. Suddenly he stops, feigns total surprise.*)

MACK. (*He always was a lousy actor.*) Mabel Normand, well of all people, hey this is some surprise!

MABEL. Mack! What are you doing here?

MACK. What does it look like, seeing people off, the Hoffmans, you heard me mention 'em, Ed and Alma, great couple, you gotta meet 'em, he's a barrel of laughs and she wears glasses. You seeing someone off too?

MABEL. Mack, didn't you know? I'm sailing!

MACK. To Europe? You? What the hell for?

MABEL. To see the sights. You may not believe it, Mr. Sennett, but there *are* things in Europe even Hollywood doesn't have. Buckingham Palace, the Louvre museum, St. Peter's in Rome . . .

MACK. A church! A big church, but a church! And no blasphemy intended, believe me I got the greatest respect for the guy, but what has the Pope got to do with making movies?

MABEL. So everything still has to do with making movies.

MACK. Well . . . (*As MUSIC of "I Won't Send Roses" comes up in piano far in the distance.*) Almost everything.

MABEL. Mack, you're making progress.

MACK. Hey, kid, you know what I was just remembering? (*Sitting next to her on trunk.*) That night about a million years ago when you first asked me that. We were on the train to California and we discovered we had some "mutual interests."

MABEL. I think I remember, Mack.

MACK. Well, kid, hold onto your hat, I'm gonna hand you a laugh.

MABEL. Shoot, boss. Always ready for a laugh.

MACK. Supposing . . . Just supposing . . . That night a million years ago I gave you the full romantic treatment! "Kid I love you, forget the napkin ring how about a real one. . ." What would you have said?

MABEL. It's hard to say, Mack. It was so long ago . . .

MACK. Not for us, kid! We're movies, we just flash back! Get rid of that fancy outfit, put you back in that little straw hat you were wearing that night . . . And Alakazam! It's 1912.

MABEL. Mack, that's movies! This is *life*. And it's 1923 and I'm on my way to Paris . . . (*Softly.*) With a friend.

MACK. Yeah, I read about your friend. Now don't get me wrong, kid, I don't hate him because he's a phoney and a bum . . . I hate him because he makes such lousy movies! (*Taking her hand.*) Aah, Mabel, let him go to Europe by himself! Come back with me! I'll even make that damn "Molly!" No Sennett touches, no Kops, no gorilla, not even a tiny little monkey. (*Then continuing enthusiastically just as* MABEL *was beginning to believe him.*) . . . Then when we get the feature out of the way I got a great idea for a new two-reeler, Mabel's Big Blast, you work in this dynamite factory see and Wally comes in selling matches. . . . (MABEL *turns away.*) What's the matter, kid? I say the wrong words again?

MABEL. You said the only words you could, Mack.

MACK. (*Realizing.*) But not the words you wanted to hear. (*There is a silence, the MUSIC stops, finally* MACK *pulls himself together.*) Well, it was a "just suppose" question anyway. To hand you a laugh. Hell it worked out fine for us the way it did. You got your friend . . . And I got my Kops. (*Rising.*) I gotta beat it, kid. Don't want old Eddie and Alma to think I forgot 'em. You have a good time in Europe . . . (*Starts Left, suddenly stops.*) And hey, if you do see the Pope you don't have to mention what I said about his church. I've seen pictures of it. Very impressive. They say you can get 4000 people inside at one time! (*The same old* MACK.) Wow, what a movie house *that* would make. (*And he starts off. Halfway out he stops, realizes he still is carrying the box of flowers. For a moment he hesitates, don't know whether to give them to* MABEL *or not, then suddenly starts out whistling to cover his emotion as he hoists the flower box over one shoulder and exits.* TAYLOR *has started down gangway through last of this. A moment, then he crosses to* MABEL.)

TAYLOR. . . . There you are, darling! Everybody's asking for you. Who was that?

MABEL. Nobody. A . . . A fan.

TAYLOR. (*Meaningfully.*) I'd say a very special fan. (MABEL *looks at him.*) I saw him, darling. You really must learn to manage these things with a bit more imagination. My red suitcase!

MABEL. Bill, I swear, I had no idea Mack was . . .

TAYLOR. I know. Coincidence. Now come along and let's get the rest of our fond farewells over with. I'll fix a little pick-me-up to get us through it.

MABEL. I don't want another drink, Bill.

TAYLOR. I agree, darling! We need something more festive for such a gala occasion. (*Taking vial from his pocket.*) A whiff of angel dust to drive away any sad thoughts from that dizzy little brain. Now take a good deep breath like Uncle Bill taught you . . . (MABEL *protests, he insists.*) Come on, be a good girl, in with the bad air, out with the good. (*And* MABEL *sniffs the powder. She closes her eyes as it begins to affect her.*) . . . Now say the magic words with me. Bye, Mack!

MABEL. (*Repeating.*) Bye, Mack.

TAYLOR. Not very convincing I'm afraid . . .

MABEL. I've only just learned the lines, Bill. (*Managing a smile.*) . . . I'll get better with practice.

TAYLOR. (*As* MABEL *takes another sniff of powder.*) Darling, I'm going to get rid of that bunch of leeches! We'll have a private sailing party of our own. Go up on the top deck and watch the lights on the water.

MABEL. (*As MUSIC comes up,* TAYLOR *starts up gangway.*) I like lights! Mack always had so many. Kleig lights, arcs, spots . . .

TAYLOR. I'm afraid this is just plain moonlight, darling. Mack's not in charge up there . . . Yet.

MABEL. (*As he exits.*) Oh but he will be. Just give him time. Just give us all . . . Time. (*And she sings.*)
TIME HEALS EVERYTHING
TUESDAY
THURSDAY
TIME HEALS EVERYTHING
APRIL
AUGUST
IF I'M PATIENT THE BREAK WILL MEND
AND ONE FINE MORNING THE HURT WILL END
SO MAKE THE MOMENTS FLY
AUTUMN

WINTER
I'LL FORGET YOU BY
NEXT YEAR
SOME YEAR
THOUGH IT'S HELL THAT I'M GOING THROUGH
SOME TUESDAY
THURSDAY
APRIL
AUGUST
AUTUMN
WINTER
NEXT YEAR
SOME YEAR
TIME HEALS EVERYTHING
TIME HEALS EVERYTHING
BUT LOVING YOU.

(*Ship's horn blows, a burst of activity as* PURSER *hurries down gangway.*)

PURSER. . . . Miss Normand, please, you must board the ship, we are about to sail! (*He helps her to gangway as he shouts "Allons, vite! On part! Depechez vous! Vite!" to Dockers as they bring last pieces of baggage on board.* TAYLOR'S FRIENDS *hurry down gangway through this. Gangway pulled off as* FRIENDS *wave and* TAYLOR *and* MABEL *appear on deck above.* TAYLOR *exits as* FRIENDS *start off.* MABEL *continues.*)

MABEL.
MAKE THE MOMENTS FLY
AUTUMN
WINTER
I'LL FORGET YOU BY
NEXT YEAR
SOME YEAR
THOUGH IT'S HELL THAT I'M GOING THROUGH
SOME TUESDAY
THURSDAY
APRIL
AUGUST
AUTUMN
WINTER
NEXT YEAR
SOME YEAR
TIME HEALS EVERYTHING

TIME HEALS EVERYTHING
BUT LOVING YOU!

(*LIGHTS down to a spot on* MABEL, *it irises out and we come
up on . . .*)

ACT TWO

SCENE 4

MACK *in hard white light Center, the rhythmic sound of taps
somewhere behind him. As he stands there a formation of*
CHORUS GIRLS *in sequinned costumes start out up Right
and Left and sweep past him.* GIRLS *strike a pose, taps
hold, as* MACK *speaks.*

MACK. . . . The hell they quit, I fired 'em! (*As* GIRLS, *in
hold position, tap lightly but steadily behind him.*) Alright,
they made it easy for me. Asked for contracts I couldn't give
'em, money I didn't have. Ella went first. (*As* ELLA *starts
down through* GIRLS.) They offered to let her head the
new music department at Universal and I wasn't going to
stand in her way.
    ELLA. (*As she exits.*) I'm sorry, Mack.
    MACK. (*As* WALLY *comes sliding, tumbling through* GIRLS.)
Then Wally found a partner who could really kick him in the
behind and they made that whole series of two-reelers for
Roach. It hurt when that sonofabitch Frank left. (FRANK
walks through GIRLS.) Quit me to go write comedies for
First National! And you know what the audience was supposed to laugh at? Lines! Not titles, lines they said to each
other on some kind of sound track some idiot said was going
to "revolutionize the industry." Hey, you know a funny thing
about Frank? (FRANK *holds.*) I think that bastard was in love
with Mabel all those years. He never said it, but I'll bet he
was just the same. (FRANK *leaves as* MABEL, *in beautiful gown,
starts on. She weaves unsteadily through* GIRLS.) Mabel
didn't leave me. She didn't have to. She just never came back.
(*As* MABEL *crosses to join* TAYLOR, *in dinner clothes, who appears Down Right.*) This was a town where everybody talked.
Even if you didn't want to listen you had to hear the rumors.
And so I knew that she was still with her friend. More than
that I didn't know. (*As* TAYLOR *leads her off.*) . . . More than
that I didn't want to know! (*Pulling himself together.*) But it

was Lottie, my broken-down hoofer, who first hit it really
big when she made the Vitagraph Varieties of 1929! Hell, if
you could say words on that screen you could sing. And if
you could sing . . . you could dance!

(*Silver ribbons drop down to form a glamorous Busby Burk-
    ley backdrop as* LOTTIE, *in black sequinned pajamas and
    a top hat, sweeps down through the* GIRLS *as MUSIC
    comes up,* MACK *exits, and she sings.*)

LOTTIE.
TAP YOUR TROUBLES AWAY
YOU'VE BOUNCED A BIG CHECK
YOUR MOM HAS THE VAPORS
TAP YOUR TROUBLES AWAY
YOUR CAR HAD A WRECK
THEY'RE SERVING YOU PAPERS
WHEN YOU'RE THE ONE THAT IT ALWAYS
    RAINS ON
SIMPLY TRY PUTTING YOUR MARY JANES ON
THE BOSS JUST GAVE YOU THE AX
THERE'S YEARS OF BACK TAX
YOU SIMPLY CAN'T PAY
IF A SKY FULL OF CRAP
ALWAYS LANDS IN YOUR LAP
MAKE A CURTSEY AND
TAP YOUR TROUBLES AWAY
        (*Tap interlude, a la Berkley, with* LOTTIE *and* GIRLS. *End
        dance chorus and* LOTTIE *continues.*)
TAP YOUR TROUBLES AWAY
YOU'RE SUED FOR DIVORCE
YOUR BROTHER GETS LOCKED UP
TAP YOUR TROUBLES AWAY
YOU'RE FAT AS A HORSE
AND FIND THAT YOU'RE KNOCKED UP
WHEN YOU NEED SOMETHING TO TURN YOUR
    MIND OFF
WHY NOT TRY TAPPING YOUR POOR BEHIND
    OFF
YOUR BOAT GOES OVER THE FALLS
THE PLANE YOU'RE ON STALLS
THE PILOT YELLS "PRAY"
WHEN YOUR PARACHUTE STRAP
IS BEGINNING TO SNAP
SMILE A BIG SMILE AND

TAP, TAP, TAP YOUR TROUBLES AWAY
> (*A second dance interlude building to climax as* LOTTIE *sings.*)

WHEN THE WOLF'S AT THE DOOR
THERE'S A BLUEBIRD IN STORE
IF YOU GLIDE CROSS THE FLOOR
TILL YOUR ANKLES GET SORE
JUST TAP YOUR TROUBLES AWAY!
> ALL GIRLS.

YOUR TROUBLES AWAY!
> LOTTIE and GIRLS.

YOUR TROUBLES AWAY!

(*End NUMBER, applause. MUSIC picks up from beginning of Second Dance Interlude as if it were a regular reprise. Terrace of* TAYLOR'S *Home comes out Down Right through this and as* GIRLS *and* LOTTIE *continue dance LIGHTS pick out party in progress at* TAYLOR'S *home.* MABEL *is high, grapples with* TAYLOR *for more "dust," he becomes irritated, slaps her, pushes her out. A disapproving* PHYLLIS FOSTER *walks out after her. Other two couples see it is time to go, hastily take their leave.* TAYLOR *is alone with* SERGE. *He laughs and puts his arm around* SERGE'S *shoulder.* SERGE *looks at him coldly,* TAYLOR *removes his arm. The two men stare at each other with ill-concealed loathing. A moment, then* SERGE *leaves.* TAYLOR *starts inside house to get another drink as* GIRLS *tap. No music. Suddenly there is a series of five rapid pistol shots from inside house. Silver ribbons crash to Stage floor as* TAYLOR *staggers out of doorway clutching his stomach and slowly sinks to the ground. Shouts of* NEWSBOYS *heard Up Right and Left in darkness, "Extra, Extra, Read all about it, William Desmond Taylor murdered!" "Extra, Extra, Famous motion picture director murdered" . . . Etc.* VOICES *fade as LIGHTS come back up on* LOTTIE *as she sings.*)

> LOTTIE.

WHEN THE WOLF'S AT THE DOOR
THERE'S A BLUEBIRD IN STORE
IF YOU GLIDE CROSS THE FLOOR
TILL YOUR ANKLES GET SORE
JUST TAP YOUR TROUBLES AWAY!
> GIRLS. (*As the start to exit.*)

YOUR TROUBLES AWAY

YOUR TROUBLES AWAY
YOUR TROUBLES AWAY
YOUR TROUBLES AWAY . . .
   LOTTIE. (*Exiting Up Center.*)
YOUR TROUBLES AWAY
AWAY!

(*A long held note, LIGHTS out, and immediately up on . . .*)

ACT TWO

SCENE 5

MACK'S *Office Left. A desk, one or two chairs. We also see corner of* MABEL'S *bedroom in shadows Right. A chaise, a small table, a screen.* MACK *is reading newspaper in chair Down Left.*

MACK. Did you read this filth?

KLEIMAN. (*Sitting at* MACK'S *desk.*) What filth?

MACK. This. (*He flings him paper.*) They start off by saying the police admit Mabel had nothing to do with that bastard Taylor's murder, then they spend the next two pages tearing her apart.

KLEIMAN. Sennett, we are not talking about Mabel, we are talking about your next picture! Which if it don't make money is also gonna be your *last* picture!

FOX. What *if?* How can it miss? Frank here is coming back to write the screenplay and here's the surprise we told you about, Mack. We got the hottest star in talkies to be in it! Lottie! Since the Varieties of 1929 number one box-office draw in the whole country!

MACK. (*Not hearing him.*) Why the hell doesn't she do something? Fight back! We still got libel laws in this country! Filthy, muckraking sonsofabitches . . .

KLEIMAN. Mack, will you be smart for once. How she gonna fight back? Sure she didn't do it but she was with him, lovers, whatever you call it, and the public don't buy that! That's why they cancelled out her last picture after two days at the Strand!

MACK. What public? A few hysterical women who haven't been laid in twenty years! She's gotta fight.

FRANK. (*Quietly.*) Okay, Mack, so she fights. Then what does she say when they start with the other things.

MACK. What other things?

FRANK. The parties, the booze . . .

MACK. Who hasn't had a few drinks, you drink, I drink . . .

FRANK. The *other* things, Mack! The powders, the "dust." She fights the papers and they got the perfect topper. The little lady sniffs dope.

MACK. (*Getting up.*) It's a lie.

FRANK. It's not a lie, Mack. I know the guy gets it for her. Taylor started her and she got to like it. Everybody knows but you. Mabel's finished, loaded up to here with heroin, an addict . . . (*He never finishes for* MACK *lunges at him shouting* "It's a Goddam lie!" *and hurls him across the desk.*)

KLEIMAN. (*As he and* Fox *frantically separate them.*) You crazy, you some kind of lunatic? You alright, Frank? (FRANK *straightens his clothes,* MACK *just stands there unable to look at him.*)

FRANK. I'm fine. I'm sorry, Mack . . . but it's time you knew the truth.

KLEIMAN. Very good, so now he knows it! Aah, let's get back to business . . .

Fox. Come on, Frank, we'll take you to lunch. (*They start out,* FRANK *starts after them. Suddenly* MACK *stops him.*)

MACK. Frank! (FRANK *stops,* MACK *turns to him, puts his arms around him. Softly.*) Oh Jesus, oh God.

KLEIMAN. (*As he exits after* Fox.) We'll meet this afternoon to talk budget, Mack. It ain't gonna be cheap, there's all that sound equipment to buy, but with Lottie's name as insurance I guess we can take the risk . . . (*They are gone.* FRANK *turns to* MACK.)

FRANK. Will I see you this afternoon, boss?

MACK. (*Shaking his head.*) Nah, Frank. What the hell do I know about pictures with words? Movies are movies, and if I'm gonna make 'em I gotta make 'em my way.

FRANK. I win my bet, I told 'em you wouldn't do it. Got one in mind, Mack?

MACK. Yeah. An old commitment I just remembered I had. And if the boys won't go for it, what the hell I'll finance the damn thing myself. (*Going to desk, taking dogeared manuscript from drawer.*) . . . I got a script, Frank. And a star. And there won't be any Sennett touches this time! Hell, ain't I made 'em laugh enough?

FRANK. More than enough, Mack. (*Starting out.*) I better go, the boys are waiting. I won't tell them the news till after they pay the check. Hey, Mack . . . (*Stopping just before he exits. Softly.*) Give her my love.

(*MUSIC comes softly up,* MACK *takes a deep breath, starts Right as LIGHTS come up on* MABEL *as she walks a bit unsteadily into bedroom.*)

MABEL. (*Visibly pulling herself together as she sees him.*) . . . Well, Mr. Sennett! This is a surprise.

MACK. (*Pretending everything is as it always was.*) Hi, kid.

MABEL. Hey, lemme look at you. Wow, you better lay off the sauce handsome, you look like hell. Which reminds me, what'll you have to drink . . .

MACK. Look, Mabel, you're busy, I'm busy, we both got no time for fooling around . . . (*A deep breath.*) I got a deal for you.

MABEL. You too? It's my week alright. I got a helluva offer yesterday. Vaudeville. They wanna bill me as Hollywood's Mystery Woman. Did She or Didn't She Do It? What do *you* think, Mack?

MACK. I'm talking about a movie, Mabel! And not just a two-reeler, it's a feature . . . (*Showing her script.*) It's called "Molly."

MABEL. Cut the comedy, Mack, I'm not in the mood.

MACK. I'm not being funny, Frank's the hottest writer in town, I own the script and I'm gonna make it!

MABEL. With me, hah. And what about the boys? Mr. Kleiman and Mr. Fox.

MACK. They're nuts about the idea! They want you as bad as I do! (*And she knows he's lying.*)

MABEL. I see. (*Then turning from him.*) Look, Mack, I appreciate your thinking of me but I'm gonna be busy for the next few months. Been talking to the guys at Paramount and Warners and . . .

MACK. (*Shouting, it's the only way he can get through.*) Look, Miss Normand, don't give me that busy for a few months crap, I know what it means! Dough! Hitting me up for a little raise! Well it won't work, you'll get your old deal and not one penny more! And furthermore I'm adding a little clause. You ain't gonna like this but I'm a man who pays his debts and I want what I'm owed paid to me!

MABEL. (*Leaping to the bait.*) You cheapskate, I don't owe you one cent . . .

MACK. Hot knockwurst on a roll, fifteen cents! (*And she remembers.*)

MABEL. The change. From the two dimes.

MACK. Forty-six dollars and fifty cents with interest. Okay A. for St. Agnes, cough it up. (*And* MABEL *laughs despite herself. Then taking his hand.*)

MABEL. Hey, Mack, one thing I gotta know. You still gonna count for me? One you turn, two you walk, three you . . .

MACK. Mabel, I gotta! It's the only way I know how to direct!

MABEL. So who's complaining? It's the only way I know how to act. (*He has taken something from his pocket.*) What's that?

MACK. A little present. They found it when they were cleaning out your old dressing room.

MABEL. Mack . . . My goddam ring . . .

MACK. What did you expect? When two people get married, even for one picture, they gotta have a ring. (*He puts it on her finger.*) Oh Desert, it is I Mabel striding across your God-damn bosom . . . (*It is too much for* MABEL, *she turns away to hide her tears.*) Hey, cut that out! If I'd of known you were going to make such a damn fuss I would've thrown the damn thing away!

MABEL. I'm sorry, Mack . . . I just can't stop . . .

MACK. Can't your fanny, you no-talent waitress! As long as you're working for Sennett you'll do as you're told! One turn! Two wipe your eyes! Three smile! (*MUSIC comes softly up.*) Four, smile. (*He takes her hands.*) Five . . . Smile . . . (*And he sings.*)

I PROMISE YOU A HAPPY ENDING
LIKE THE ONES THAT YOU SEE ON THE SCREEN
SO IF YOU'VE HAD A BAD BEGINNING
LOVE WILL COME OUT WINNING
IN THE CLOSING SCENE
AND WHEN YOU FIND IT ROUGH CONTENDING
WITH THE GRIND THAT THE WORLD PUTS US
    THROUGH
I CAN PROMISE YOU A HAPPY ENDING
THAT HAS YOU
LOVING ME
LOVING YOU

    (*LIGHTS have begun fading on* MABEL *through this and* MACK *slowly changes his focus from her to us as he continues.*)

I PROMISE YOU A HAPPY ENDING
LIKE THE ONE YOU'VE BEEN DREAMING ABOUT
WHERE VOWS ARE VOWED
AND KNOTS ARE KNOTTED
AND THE PREACHER'S POTTED
AS THE REEL RUNS OUT
AND SO I'M STRONGLY RECOMMENDING

THAT YOU PACK UP YOUR OLD POINT OF VIEW
I CAN PROMISE YOU A HAPPY ENDING
THAT HAS YOU
LOVING ME
LOVING YOU . . .
(MABEL *has slowly walked off through this, stopping just once
to turn and look back at* MACK, *then disappearing. MUSIC
continues softly under as* MACK, *now back in the studio as he
was at the beginning of the play, turns to us.*) . . . We got
through somehow. I hocked the studio, made the picture . . .
And then those bastards wouldn't even release it! Then on
February 23, 1930, Mabel Normand died. And that's the way
the real story ended. (*Suddenly, passionately.*) But not for
me! Never for me! Because as long as there's a projector and
a foot of film and a screen up there to show it on she's alive!
And young! And beautiful. So damn their dates and damn
their facts and let me show you how Mack Sennett would
have ended this story. . . . If only life had been a movie.
(*As tinkly PIANO begins to come up softly in the distance.*)
Hell, what's life for if an artist can't change it. (*Suddenly
shouting.*) Andy, get that chapel on! And some flowers! And
where the hell's that preacher. . . .

(*LIGHTS come up as PIANO picks up tempo and volume
and we see* FRANK, LOTTIE, WALLY, ELLA, KLEIMAN, FOX,
ALL *in silent movie style as* GUESTS *at a big wedding.*
MACK *is the groom with flower in his buttonhole [which
squirts water incidentally] and finally* MABEL *in a beautiful wedding gown is brought on by* ALL *the* KEYSTONE
KOPS. *A brief ceremony,* MACK *puts the napkin ring on*
MABEL'S *finger, lets the* PREACHER *have it with a custard
pie, then the happy couple kiss and start down the long
sunlit road that stretches far away to the horizon. The
others have gone off by now, the two figures are alone,
silhouetted hand in hand against the sky. The LIGHTS
fade. The PIANO fades. And that's the end of the show.*)

PROPERTY LIST

Preset Act One—Stage Left:
ironing board (tied with trick string to collapse)
Mack's hat
mangle—rolling (Laundry Scene)
large flashlight (Watchman)
plate with sandwich—real (Mabel first entrance)
5 newspapers (stapled at corners so they won't mess Stage)
director's chair
barber cloth
scissors, comb, brush 2 dry towels (for Barber and Mack after *Pies*)
17 pies made with *crazy foam* (bought in toy shops for kids spread on
   cardboard pie dishes . . . strong dishes *not* floppy!)
rolling pie table (to hold above pies—made to conceal pies)
door knocker set up for Mack Upstage (show opening)
6 towels (100's of girls)
several chairs for "Hollywood Hotel" Scene

Act Two:
leather arm chair (Mack's Office)
bentwood chair (Mack's Office)
desk with blotter, inkwell, calendar, folded newspapers and *Script* in
   drawer
bathtub unit
bathtub screen (to hide Mack's getting undressed)
bar unit with stool on top (Mack's Office)
white flower basket with one helium filled ballon in flower arrangement
   (brought on during Scene of decorating for Mabel's return—ballon
   used by Mabel during "Mabel into the room")
horseshoe of roses (decorating Pre-Mabel Scene)
3 foam rubber covered Kop clubs (made by covering foam club with
   mens' knee length black stocking and taped at end)
1 steamer trunk
Additional:
3 rolling tables, round, with lavender table clothes for Hollywood Hotel
   Scene (Mabel rides on one during number)
5 column bases topped with palms to make Hollywood Hotel Scene
hot dog push cart (with hot dog, roll and mustard spreader) for 100's
   of girls)
leather hat box (Lottie)
vial for Mabel to sniff stuff (Sailing Scene)
box (fancy) of roses (never opened)—Mack . . . Sailing Scene

Preset Act One—Stage Right:
desk (Mack's)
3 twenty-four inch stools

rolling wardrobe hamper (Big Time)
camera with megaphone
washtub with playing cards inside and rubber baby (Laundry Scene)
rolling piano with beer stein and clothes line with clothes
2 sections of revolving drum with canvas covering and flats (Canvas covering for Big Time and Flats for Laundry Scene)
buzz saw (Big Time)
old hand projector (Look what happened . . .)
Roman table with dressing—4 goblets covered with ground cloth to protect Stage floor from "Crazy Foam" pies mess)
4 Roman stools
carton (Big Time)
observations unit of train with 2 captain's chairs
train compartment unit with phono, wax cylinder, sterno cooker, pot, silver ware, napkins, napkin ring, canned pears in pot, wooden spoon, apron (Mabel) kitchen matches
4 suitcases
4 briefcases
2 beachballs
1 birdcage (Ella, Big Time)
2 loaded blank pistols
typewriter (Frank, Big Time, etc.)
net shopping bag (Mabel. Big Time)
2 cans film (going to location
script (Frank)
red carpet (arrival in L A)
paper bag with bun (Mabel-Frank Scene)
2 rolling movie reflectors (Going on location Scene)
railroad signal (rolling) Train Scene
pushbroom covered with damp towel to clean up Pie Mess
Newspapers (Frank)
Act Two:
outdoor ballustrade (Taylor's Terrace)
fancy chair (Mabel's room)
chaise lounge (Mabel's room)
desk chair (Mack's office)
3 fold screen on push plate (Mabel's room)
2 large banners (Welcome Mabel)
white 36 inch stool
siren (Sound for Murder)
10 foam rubber covered police clubs
whiskey flask (Taylor—Sailing Scene)
boat ticket
clipboard (Ship's Purser)
gangplank unit (Scenery)
many pieces luggage
silver tray with champagne glasses (Pre Murder Scene)
Preset—Act One—Onstage:
the battery operated camera crane unit with camera
the worklight

THE SEA HORSE
EDWARD J. MOORE
(Little Theatre) Drama
1 Man, 1 Woman, Interior

It is a play that is, by turns, tender, ribald, funny and suspenseful. Audiences everywhere will take it to their hearts because it is touched with humanity and illuminates with glowing sympathy the complexities of a man-woman relationship. Set in a West Coast waterfront bar, the play is about Harry Bales, a seaman, who, when on shore leave, usually heads for "The Sea Horse," the bar run by Gertrude Blum, the heavy, unsentimental proprietor. Their relationship is purely physical and, as the play begins, they have never confided their private yearnings to each other. But this time Harry has returned with a dream: to buy a charter fishing boat and to have a son by Gertrude. She, in her turn, has made her life one of hard work, by day, and nocturnal love-making; she has encased her heart behind a facade of toughness, utterly devoid of sentimentality, because of a failed marriage. Irwin's play consists in the ritual of "dance" courtship by Harry of Gertrude, as these two outwardly abrasive characters fight, make up, fight again, spin dreams, deflate them, make love and reveal their long locked-up secrets.

"A burst of brilliance!"—*N.Y. Post.* "I was touched close to tears!"—*Village Voice.* "A must! An incredible love story. A beautiful play?"—*Newhouse Newspapers.* "A major new playwright!"—*Variety.*

ROYALTY, $50-$35

THE AU PAIR MAN
HUGH LEONARD
(Little Theatre) Comedy
1 Man, 1 Woman, Interior

The play concerns a rough Irish bill collector named Hartigan, who becomes a love slave and companion to an English lady named Elizabeth, who lives in a cluttered London town house, which looks more like a museum for a British Empire on which the sun has long set. Even the door bell chimes out the national anthem. Hartigan is immediately conscripted into her service in return for which she agrees to teach him how to be a gentleman rather after the fashion of a reverse Pygmalion. The play is a wild one, and is really the never-ending battle between England and Ireland. Produced to critical acclaim at Lincoln Center's Vivian Beaumont Theatre.

ROYALTY, $50-$35